FALLON'S FLAW

Bullard's Battle
Book #6

Dale Mayer

FALLON'S FLAW (BULLARD'S BATTLE, BOOK 6)
Dale Mayer
Valley Publishing

Copyright © 2021

This is a work of fiction. Names, characters, places, brands, media, and incidents either are the product of the author's imagination or are used fictitiously. Any resemblance to actual events, locales, or persons, living or dead, is entirely coincidental.

ISBN-13: 978-1-773363-34-9
Print Edition

Books in This Series:

About This Book

Welcome to a new stand-alone but interconnected series from Dale Mayer. This is Bullard's story—and that of his team's. All raw, rough, incredibly capable men who have one goal: to find out who was behind the attack on their leader, before the attacker, or attackers, return to finish the job.

Stay tuned for more nonstop action as the men narrow down their suspects … and find a way to let love back into their own empty lives.

Fallon returns to Africa and Bullard's home base to follow the only active lead they have in their hunt for their plane saboteur. Once home, Fallon finds Dave, Bullard's right-hand man, heading out to check on a lead for Bullard, and Dave's niece, Linny, is home for a visit. Fallon and Linny have shared both good and bad moments, as the two of them dance around a long-term attraction—which Fallon refuses to pursue, not wanting his relationship with Bullard and the crew at the compound to change.

Linny plans to confront Fallon but instead finds an old beau dropped dead on the front steps of the compound, considered her second home. Uncle Dave is everything to her, and Bullard sent her to medical school, yet it's Fallon she keeps coming back to see.

As her world implodes, the same issues facing Fallon take a turn for the worse, … putting them all in danger.

Sign up to be notified of all Dale's releases here!
https://smarturl.it/DaleNews

CHAPTER 1

F ALLON CARTER WALKED into the main hall of Bullard's big compound, the original one in Africa, dropped his bag, placed his hands on his hips, and looked around. He smiled and murmured, "Home," to the empty room. But even that sounded and felt strange. A hollowness permeated the room, the space around him. He frowned, not sure whether it was because it lacked Bullard or because something had changed while he was away. Africa had been home to Fallon for a long time, but this was the first time it felt wrong.

"Dave, are you here?" he called out, then walked into the kitchen. There he found Dave, with a checklist and several bags at his feet.

Dave looked up in surprise. "You're earlier than I thought you'd be," he said.

"Seems like I'm just in time. What's going on here?" he asked, as he motioned at the bags. "I made good time coming in from the airport. Where are you going?" He spied the full coffeepot, headed around the large island counter, and poured himself a cup. Coming back around, he saw an odd look on Dave's face. "Talk to me," he said, his voice sharp. "Do you have news on Bullard?"

"No," he said slowly. "We do have word that somebody may have been picked up out of the water—"

"But no confirmation that it's Bullard, right? I imagine, out in that area, an awful lot of drownings and potential drownings are to be found, particularly with the refugee issue."

"And that's why we don't have any real confirmation," he said. "But my underground network says that a couple men were picked up over the last few months."

"And?"

"And I'll go check to make sure," he said. "I'll probably be gone a few days."

"It'll probably take you that long just to find out where these men are," he said. "On the other hand, it's good news that there's anything to check out. Do you want me to come?"

"No," Dave said. "I hate to even leave here, but, if one of those men is Bullard, we need to know."

"Hell yes," Fallon said forcefully. "I just don't like the idea of you going alone."

He chuckled. "And I don't like the idea of leaving you here alone."

At that, Fallon looked around and asked, "Am I alone?"

"Not quite," said a woman from the doorway.

Fallon turned to see Lindsey, Dave's niece, her arms crossed over her chest, as she leaned against the doorjamb. Fallon stared at her in surprise. "What, school's out?"

"School's been out for a while," she said, with a quirk of her lips. "I go back in September."

"So you've got some time off, is that it?" He looked at Dave. "Is it safe to leave her here alone?"

Dave's lips quirked. "Well, I was kind of hoping that she could help look after you and that you could help look after her."

"I can't babysit," Fallon said. "Quinn's on his way to meet me."

"It's not a case of babysitting," Dave protested.

"Save your breath, Dave," Lindsey said. "You know perfectly well that Fallon sees me as a little girl."

"You're well past the little-girl stage. You're a doctor, for Christ's sake," Dave muttered under his breath.

"It won't matter to Fallon, who thinks education isn't of any value if it doesn't come hand in hand with experience," she said.

"I never said that," Fallon said, rolling his eyes.

"Well"—she sighed—"that's all it's ever been for you anyway."

He sighed, looked at Dave, and asked, "How long will you be gone again?"

Dave chuckled. "It won't be that big of a deal," he said. "The two of you will get along just fine."

Just then the front door opened, and footsteps could be heard coming down the long hallway. Fallon smiled. "That'll be Quinn." He felt the relief washing through him, knowing he wouldn't be alone with Lindsey now. He'd always called her Linny Brat. But, in truth, she was Dave's niece, now about twenty-eight or twenty-nine years old. And too damn attractive for her own good.

Just enough heat existed between the two of them that Fallon had deliberately held back on his feelings because he didn't want to screw things up here for himself. He'd met way too many people who had changed their own pathways because of relationships, and, if Lindsey was intent on being a practicing doctor, the last thing Fallon wanted to do was change that. He had seen the dedication and the purpose in her over the years, but they'd only crossed paths at the compound off and on for a week or two, occasionally three weeks at a time. Then he was off again, gone on missions, and she was here. The frustration and irritation between them confirmed that he should continue keep his distance, if he didn't want to change the status quo completely.

"Hello," Quinn called out, walking into the kitchen, where he heard the voices. As soon as he saw Linny, he opened his arms, and she ran into them, the two of them chuckling with joy at seeing each other.

Fallon often wondered why she didn't have that same relationship with him. From the look on Dave's face, as Dave studied Fallon's own expression, Fallon realized that Dave knew more than he was letting on. Fallon glared at his old friend. "If you're not gone for too long," he said easily, "it won't make much difference if we get along or not."

"I hope it won't take me long," he said, "but I need to know enough to confirm whether anything's out there on Bullard or not. If there's any chance ..."

"We need to know, for all of us," Fallon said.

Quinn turned and asked, "What am I missing?"

"There's been word of a few men picked up out of the ocean," Dave said.

"Bullard?" Quinn asked, his voice excited, yet sharp with fear.

"Nobody knows, and none of the pictures are clear enough to identify him." Dave sighed. "A couple could possibly be him, but, at the same time, it depends on how long he's been out there."

"It's been a long time," Quinn said. "He shouldn't still be in the ocean."

"Exactly, but I can't *not* go," Dave said.

Immediately Quinn nodded. "Absolutely. We'll be here

and keep everything running while you're gone. We'll also look after little Linny here for you."

"Well, *little Linny here*," Lindsey said, with a half laugh, "is just fine and was planning on looking after you guys."

"We're both old hands in the kitchen," Quinn said easily. "But, if you've got some of your uncle's special treats, you know that we'll be up for that."

"Is it always about sweets?"

"Always," he confirmed immediately.

She smiled, looked at Uncle Dave, and said, "See? I told you that I'd be fine."

He nodded and shot a sideways glance at Fallon. "In that case," he said, "with you guys here early, I can get to the airport sooner myself. I wouldn't mind having a little bit of a breather, just in case."

"Do you want a ride?" Fallon asked.

"No," he said. "I'm just taking a car and leaving it at the airport."

"Good enough," he said.

With that, Lindsey gave her uncle a quick hug, while Fallon watched.

Fallon said, "Seems like one of us is always walking out the door."

"We are," Dave said. "And it's been quite a bit worse lately. Check in on the big console to see where everybody is. I've left detailed notes. Plus, the guys in Australia have a good idea of who is where and what's been happening."

"Is there anything we need to know?"

"Linny already knows. She's been acting as my command central assistant for the most part," he said, glancing at his watch. "It's later than I thought," he said worriedly, as he snatched his bags and raced to the front door.

"I can drive you," Quinn said. "I'll get you there faster." Dave stopped, looked at him, and frowned. Quinn took over the decision-making and said, "Come on. I'll be back home again in a couple hours. It'll take Fallon that long to get settled in anyway."

"Hardly," he said. "You know us. We hit the ground running." But he was talking to empty air because Quinn was already racing out the front door to get Dave to the airport. Sipping his coffee, Fallon sat here for a few moments, studying the empty doorway. He turned and looked at Lindsey. "Anybody else around?"

"Nope, nobody at all," she said.

"Any danger of attack here? Anything strange since Bullard's disappearance?"

She turned, stared at him for a long moment, and said, "No, nothing."

"That's almost more disconcerting," he said.

"It is?" she asked. "I don't deal as intimately with the workings of the company as you do, but I know Uncle Dave's been worried."

"With good reason," he muttered. "We don't know whether somebody is trying to take over the company to put it out of business or to implement some other nefarious scheme they've dreamed up in their head, or whatever."

"But somebody has to know something. I can't believe you guys haven't found any answers yet."

He immediately took offense. "It's not like we've had a whole lot of time."

"You've had weeks," she pointed out.

He glared at her. "Thanks for reminding me." He picked up his coffee cup, topped it off, then headed toward their big command center. She followed him. He didn't really mind that, yet, at the same time, her comment had hit a sore spot. He asked her, "Was everything really connected to that last asshole out of France?"

"If it is, it makes no sense. So far, all we're doing is finding various heads of the legendary Greek Hydra, but we haven't found out who's behind it all."

"So, in other words, somebody has laid a pretty good trail, leading off in a lot of different directions."

"But," she quipped, "it's closer, another rung up the ladder, so it shouldn't be too hard for you guys to find him."

"Well, you'd think so," he said. "The question is, what's behind it though? Because we don't have a tangible target. We thought we did with Kingdom Securities—and had some ideas before that—and maybe it still is partly from that corner, but we don't know enough yet."

"I presume you've tracked bank accounts and things like that," she asked.

"I'll check in with the Australian team to see where they're at with it," he said. "But, from what I understand, that's what they're working on. Among other things."

"Right," she muttered. She stared at the map that showed all their team members all over the place. "I don't even know how Uncle Dave keeps track of all this."

"Very carefully," he said, with a half smile. "He knows every one of us really well, and I'm sure he'd like to keep us close."

"With good reason," she said admittedly. "But, with Bullard missing, that's hit him the hardest."

"Bullard's loss has hit all of us," he said. "I'm trying hard not to be a pessimist about it, but it's not easy."

"Well, that was always one of your flaws, wasn't it?"

"One of?" he asked in a sardonic tone.

"Well, you're often pessimistic about things."

"I wouldn't have thought so," he said, protesting.

"I would," she said, with a shrug.

"*Huh*," he said, not knowing how else to respond.

She smiled and changed the subject. "Dinner is already in the oven. I put it in, knowing you guys were coming in after a lot of traveling. I'll go throw in a pie or something to go with it."

He looked at her, surprised. "Is dinner that easy for you?"

She nodded. "Keeping track of all these guys isn't."

He looked back at the console and nodded. "Yeah, it can be difficult at times."

"Putting a pie in the oven is easy," she said, then walked away, leaving him alone. He watched as she disappeared, wondering at this woman, who seemed capable of handling so many different aspects of life. She hadn't had it easy. Her parents had been murdered by a terrorist on the streets in a car bombing. Dave had immediately swooped in, picked her up, and brought her here. Everybody had immediately coddled her. She'd been what? Fifteen or sixteen? Too old for all the coddling but too young to be on her own.

She'd been very driven by the world that they lived in, not wanting to be touched by it, yet unable to stay away from it. She'd always kept herself at a distance, watching as they operated, realizing that what they did was valuable, yet still she was frustrated because nobody had been there in time to save her parents. Fallon could never change that, since they hadn't even known about it until it happened. They later discovered that her father had been targeted, and Bullard's teams had carefully made sure that the culprit was taken care of.

That had helped Lindsey to heal and to see what they did as having as much value as anything else in the world. Then she had turned to medicine, and they'd all been grateful because it gave her an outlet like nothing else. She'd been laser focused on it, an interest that just never quit.

Fallon had worked for Bullard for a long time now. He didn't remember exactly when he'd come on board, but it was before Linny lost her parents. So quite a long time ago. He'd been back and forth, come and gone. He hadn't been here at the immediate start of Bullard's security business, but Fallon had come on board soon afterward. He found himself wondering just how long ago it had been but didn't want to bring up some of the pain she'd been through by asking her.

The loss of Bullard right now affected them all, bringing up memories that they didn't want. Fallon had to continue to wait until they found a lead, and then he would be up and gone himself. Now he wanted that because he could actually do something. Maybe they needed to bring in some more of the team; yet he didn't want to leave Linny here alone. Fallon would argue that nobody would head out in these scenarios without backup. But there was no backup for Linny.

Pondering that, he sent Dave a text. **What if we have to leave?**

Dave immediately answered, **Leave her behind.**

Easy to say, he wrote. **But not without backup. We need to bring some of the team back from Australia.**

No, they're the ones who gave me the leads on these men, he typed. **We can't afford to do that.**

We can't have her in danger.

Are you expecting an attack?

I'm not expecting an attack, but I can't *not* expect

to be attacked either, he clarified. **Anywhere within my circle could put her in trouble.**

Dave sent back, **Maybe I shouldn't have left.**

No, he typed. **You are one who can find him.** Dave had the mannerisms of somebody who was much less aggressive. He could be infinitely more dangerous than people expected, since he was as well-trained as the rest of them. Fallon had an awful lot of history that was pretty hard to walk away from, but he also understood that no way he wanted to leave Lindsey alone. **I'll find a way around it**, Fallon typed.

I can't have her hurt, Dave wrote.

No, he typed, **neither can I.** At that, Dave sent him a little heart emoji. Fallon stared at it and frowned. Still he wished Dave well. If anybody could ferret out where Bullard might be hiding, it would be Dave.

BAKING WAS SOMETHING she could do blindfolded. Lindsey hated to admit just how much seeing Fallon again affected her. They'd had this truce, where she allowed him to look at her as a little kid and to bug her the same way, but she was damn tired of it. She'd lost her virginity a hell of a long time ago and had spent time with somebody who she thought had been important, only to realize afterward that he had been a blip on the radar, when her focus had come back to that damn Fallon—the one guy she couldn't stop thinking about.

She was hug-friendly with everybody else here, but, with Fallon, they kept a wary distance. She figured it was because, one day, they would go up in flames together. She couldn't wait for that day, but he seemed determined to keep her at arm's length.

She had talked to her uncle about it a couple times, and

he'd explained how Fallon struggled with some things—one being breaking up a family unit by having a relationship with somebody close to the family. She didn't quite understand that but figured that it went along with stepbrothers not wanting to have relationships with stepsisters or not having a relationship with your best friend because you were afraid of losing that initial friendship. And she understood that, but, at the same time, they were adults, and, if this was something they both wanted, they should certainly go for it.

But then the woman inside her was desperate to have this relationship. She felt like she'd been waiting and waiting since forever. She kept coming back here after her semesters, if she wasn't doing various trainings, though it seemed like her entire world was training.

She needed to take as many breaks as she could because her medical school schedule was deadly. But she was struggling with that as would anybody. She could only do what she could do, but it was hard sometimes. Still, seeing Fallon here was one thing, but realizing that he didn't want her here was another.

She understood that the company was in turmoil, with Bullard missing and presumably dead, not to mention the assaults against other team members. They were trying to keep a lid on the news globally, as far as she understood from her uncle. It was easy to see that tension in the air when she came home this time. Her uncle was visibly rattled, and, though he was holding it together, when he gave himself a moment to unwind, the grief he felt was evident.

It was too early for everybody to determine that Bullard was *gone*, gone, but she understood that their business tended to make the disappearances seriously hard accept. The fact that two men had survived the plane crash was enough to keep hope alive, though, in this case, she wasn't sure hope was something they should keep alive.

How many more trips like this would her uncle make? Always looking for that one threadbare line of hope that he could tug to see if, by any chance, he found Bullard there. She then realized that Uncle Dave was nowhere near ready to walk away. She understood that she really did, but it was just so damn hard to see anyone suffer; and they were all suffering here.

This had been one of the things that had always amazed her about this "family" because they were all so damn close. She had only ever seen one other like it, and that was at Levi and Ice's compound. Linny had gone there once, or maybe twice, though she had to think about that. She had seen them here several times. She'd been doing a practicum in Houston and had stopped in for a few days. She'd thoroughly enjoyed that visit, meeting friends again, old and new.

She knew that they were working as hard as anyone to find Bullard too. Theirs was a weird relationship, which she didn't quite understand—between Bullard, Levi, and Ice. Uncle Dave had just smiled and said that love took many forms. She wasn't sure whether that was a cop-out or Bullard really had been in love with Ice. Yet she absolutely adored Levi, so it was kind of hard to see how that would all work. But Linny felt sorry for Bullard, if that were the case.

Sometimes though, one had to force the hand of what was going on in their world in order to make progress happen. While she was busy rolling out pie dough, feeling eyes on her, she looked up to find Fallon leaning against the doorway. "Well, did you solve the problems of the world?" she asked, as she turned her attention to a bag of apples.

He watched as she peeled and sliced them. "That looks

really good."

"Yes," she said in a dry tone. "Amazing, isn't it? I can actually bake."

He looked at her in surprise. "You've always pulled off wicked desserts."

"I'm not just another housewife in the making," she said in a dry tone.

"No, according to Dave, you are one hell of a surgeon."

"Well, I will be," she said, "but I've got a lot of surgeries to get through first."

"And I thought you were about to become a doctor."

"No, that was two years ago," she said cheerfully. "I am a doctor already. Now I am trying to get my surgical practicum completed as well."

"What kind of surgery?"

"Not sure yet," she said. "An awful lot of choices are out there. But I'll probably specialize in general surgery."

He nodded. "Interesting choice."

"Well, it's not as if I haven't seen my fair share of gunshot wounds," she quipped.

"And we appreciate your service," he said more formally.

She studied him quietly. "You do know that there's not a very good chance of Bullard surviving, right?"

"Sure. We all know that," he said, his tone easy and relaxed. "But we also know him, and we're holding out hope."

"That's the problem with hope," she said. "It keeps things alive, well past the point that they probably should be."

"I think it'll take a lot longer than a few weeks for us to walk away from this."

"Got it," she said. "I just feel bad for my uncle."

"He's pretty affected by it, isn't he?"

"Yes, I'd forgotten how close they were."

"Well, Bullard pulled your uncle out of a really bad patch way back when," he said. "So it makes sense."

"Maybe," she said, "but death is death, and grief and loss are hard on us all."

"I think it's harder on civilians because they feel helpless to do anything, not having been trained, like us," he said. "I would love to see Bullard step through those doors, as hale and hearty has ever," he said. "But it's hard to imagine at this point."

"Exactly," she said. "I see death on a daily basis, and that's pretty damn hard to deal with too."

"And yet you chose it. How come?"

She appreciated the questioning tone in his voice; it wasn't a complete judgment call. It seemed like he was trying to understand.

"I did choose it," she said, "because, so many times, we pull people back from the brink of death or improve the quality of their lives. I feel like I'm doing something constructive to help the world out there, and I don't want to stop."

"Do you ever think you'll get tired of it?"

"I'm sure I will," she said. "But hopefully there'll be another case, where I feel like I can make a difference."

"And that's what it's all about, isn't it?" he said, with a quirk of his lips.

She looked up in surprise, as she tossed sugar and cornstarch and cinnamon over her apples. "What do you mean?"

"It's all about making a difference in the world," he murmured.

"Isn't that why you do what you do?" she asked.

"It is, I suppose," he said. "I just don't usually put it in those terms."

"Maybe you should," she said, with a smile.

"Maybe, but again it's not necessarily something I think about."

"It would have put you on this pathway a long time ago," she said.

"The question is, what difference would it have made at that point?"

CHAPTER 2

F ALLON HAD LONG since left to go do whatever it was
that he did, and Linny sat, hovering over a pie, wondering at how different her world was every time she came here.
Suddenly a security alarm sounded, and she spun around and
stared.

Fallon called to her, "Don't open the door."

"Wasn't planning on it," she murmured, as she stared at
the front door.

"Come into the back, please."

"What is it?"

"One of the outside alarms has been triggered."

"It happened a few days ago too," she muttered.

He gave her a hard look.

"I didn't know what it was," she said. "They told me it
wasn't anything important."

"I wonder if they would agree with that now," he murmured. Just then his phone rang. "Quinn, where are you?"
he asked.

"I'm about ten minutes out," he said. "Just before I left
Dave, he told me something had been going on with the
alarm system."

"Like what? Because it's just gone off," he said. "Any
idea what it is?"

"No," he responded. "He just said that it's been going

off at odd hours."

"A short in the line?"

"Or somebody testing it."

"Yeah, I don't like the sound of that," Fallon said.

"No, I don't either. I'm booking it now, so about seven minutes out."

"Okay, I'll go check it out," he said.

"Or you could wait until I get in," he said.

"That's the problem with just the two of us here," he stated. "I need to go check this out now, but I don't want to leave Lindsey alone." He heard her, as she gasped. He turned and glared at her.

"Well, the cameras should be up and running, and he's also got a new system," Quinn said.

"I was just trying to figure that out, when the alarm went off. It seems like we have two cameras outside, and one more at the north end of the driveway. That's new."

"Right. Have you checked them to see what's going on?"

"I'm trying to bring them online, but they're not coming up."

"Well, give me five more minutes to get there, and we'll do a full check."

"I also need to check what the armory is looking like now. I think Dave's struggling, keeping up with everything."

"I'm sure he has," Quinn said. "Almost there." And he hung up.

She looked at him and said, "You're not blaming my uncle for this."

"I'm not blaming your uncle for anything. Maintaining a place like this is a ton of work in the best of times," he said. "So I can't really say who, what, when, or anything else about what's going on, but, if we have an intruder, I want to make sure he doesn't get in through the normal methods."

"You want him to get in another way?" she asked curiously.

"I don't want him to get in at all," he said, with a half smile. "But I also don't know how the armory is stocked right now."

"Is that really the most important issue?"

"No, it sure isn't," he said. "What is important is that you stay safe. So I'll check the armory, and then I'll do a full sweep outside."

Just then the alarm stopped.

"You see? I don't like that," he said. "Anything creepy like that just gets my back up."

She turned to glare at him, but he was gone. She returned to the kitchen and checked her pie, thinking about it. Uncle Dave had explained that a bunch of glitches were going on, but, with everything else, the others were more edgy over a security system that wouldn't stop sending out alarms. It didn't mean that any answers were here to be found, but she also couldn't be sure that there weren't, either.

As she pulled out the pie and set it on the counter, she looked out and thought she caught sight of somebody walking outside the building. She frowned, took off her oven mitts, and walked to the window to take a closer look, but nobody was there. She pulled out her phone, checked the contacts that she needed—because, of course, she had everybody's just in case, and always had. That was Uncle Dave's doing, making sure she was safe and had other resources besides him. She sent Fallon a message. **Are you outside the kitchen?**

He replied with **No.**

Somebody just walked by, she texted.

Immediately he sent a message. **I'm on it.**

She moved from window to window, searching to see if she could catch sight of the stranger again. But nothing. She got a message back a few moments later.

Any other sign?

She texted back, **No.**

Coming in.

She walked back to the kitchen, frowning. Was it possible she'd imagined it? Would they really get attacked here? Nothing seemed sensible about it. As she turned around in the kitchen, she almost shrieked. Standing in front of her was Quinn. He grabbed her shoulders and said, "It's okay. Sorry. I didn't mean to scare you."

"You might not have meant to," she told him, "but you sure as hell did."

He smiled again and said, "Sorry."

"We thought we saw somebody outside," she said. He looked at her in surprise. She shrugged. "Fallon's out looking."

He spun around. "Where?"

She pointed to the window and said, "I thought I saw somebody. It wasn't you, was it?"

"No," he said. "I'll go out and take a look."

"Or not," she said, "because Fallon already is."

"Yeah, well, I think I'll go take a quick look anyway." And, with that, he disappeared.

She stared out the same kitchen window, until she saw him approach the spot where she thought she'd seen somebody. He did a quick search around and kept expanding the area. She appreciated his thoroughness, but then she hadn't even heard him come inside. And that bothered her more. It's like he had gliders on his feet or something. She sat back, a little more on edge than she'd expected.

When the two men both came in together, she looked up and asked, "So was it just my imagination?"

"Don't know about that," Fallon said, "but no sign of anyone out there now."

"Well, that's a good thing," she murmured.

"It is, but, at the same time, we have to be vigilant. If anything like this happens again, make sure you tell us."

She shrugged.

Fallon glared at her. "No, don't brush it off," he said. "Bullard is missing. So far five of us have been attacked. We're at war. We don't know with whom, and we don't know why. But somebody is out there and is coming after us."

"No," she corrected. "They went after Bullard and what? Five team members? But the initial plane crash was about Bullard and Ryland and Garret. You still don't even know yet whether the attackers were after the team members or Bullard."

"We've looked at the issue of Garret or Ryland being the target and didn't find anything," he murmured.

"So you've narrowed it down to just being Bullard?"

"Yes," they both said.

"But there have been threats against the whole team as well, so we don't really know. This kind of work creates enemies," Fallon said.

"Damn," she said. "Because it would be nice to think that other hypothetical options were here." She paused a moment. "More than that," she snapped, after a moment of frustration. "I hate to see that somebody might have succeeded."

"We're not too thrilled with the concept either," Quinn said, "but we don't know what the end game is."

"Well, if they take out Bullard, this property still belongs to whoever is in his will, right?"

"In theory, yes," Fallon said, with a glance at Quinn, "and we don't know the information around that legality. Also, if no body is found, Bullard must be declared dead, and that can take many, many, years. Especially in a situation like this."

"So maybe the end game is confusion and chaos, ultimately bringing down the company?"

"Quite possibly, yes." Fallon nodded. "It could also just be somebody who wanted him gone and doesn't give a shit about anything else."

"I get that," she said. "It still sucks. Also, by the way, I'm only supposed to be here for a couple days. Then I'm heading back to New York."

"Got it," he said. "I'm sorry you can't spend it with your uncle."

"Me too," she said. "He would have stayed, if I'd asked him to, but I can come another time."

"Understood," Fallon said, as he looked at her. "And you don't have to leave because he's not here either, though."

"Good," she said. "And that's not why I'm leaving." But she didn't offer anything else.

FALLON REFUSED TO ask any more questions. If she wanted him to know something else, she would have said more. But, at the same time, he felt his heart sinking at the thought of her leaving again. It seemed like they were always like this, ships in the night, but never actually sitting at the same dock long enough to really get to know each other. He felt Quinn's intense gaze, but he refused to look at him. "I'll go see if we have any alerts and what comes up on the cameras," he said.

"Didn't you have cameras up while you were out there?" she asked in surprise.

He shook his head. "I was trying to get it all fixed up, before I went out. I don't know if it worked or not." He headed to the control center, Quinn at his side.

"You didn't see anything, did you?" Quinn asked.

"I didn't, and that kind of bothers me too," he said. "None of this makes any sense. But then I've said that a million times already."

"Got it, and, just like the rest of us, you're frustrated."

"We all are," he murmured.

"Interesting though," he said, "that you have the relationship you do with her."

"What relationship?" he asked bluntly.

At that, Quinn chuckled. "Exactly. The two of you keep dancing around each other, but neither one of you is willing to take that step."

"It's not good business," Fallon said.

"Bullshit," Quinn said. "You're well past that stage."

"We'll never get past that stage," he said, reaching the console and clicking to look at the monitors. "She's Dave's niece. I'm not screwing things up here because of that."

"That's not a good reason," he murmured. "It's not like she's seventeen or something. She's an intelligent, independent adult in her own right. I think that's more of an excuse."

At that, Fallon stiffened. "Whatever." Quinn could think what he wanted, regardless.

"You always were narrow-minded, very black-and-white.

You stay focused on what you want and ignore anything else."

"Since when is that a problem?" he murmured.

"It's not a problem, but it can, in some situations, be a fatal flaw."

"Bullshit," he said good-naturedly. "It's that very intensity that gets us what we need a lot of the time."

"That's true," he said, "but, sometimes, it's just a little much."

Fallon glared at him. "Are you telling me that I'm missing something?"

"No, I wouldn't dare," he said, chuckling. "Come on. Let's go back to work."

But he hadn't actually moved away from work, so he didn't quite understand what the beef was. "I don't see anything," Fallon said, after scanning multiple monitors.

"What's that?" Quinn asked, as he tapped something on the screen.

Fallon narrowed the frame, bringing it into closer alignment. "Looks like a stick maybe?"

"Yet, it wasn't there when I went outside," Quinn said.

"*Huh*," he said, as he stared at it for a long moment. "I wonder if somebody thinks she's here alone."

"Now that's an interesting possibility. Maybe they saw me leave with Dave and his bags."

"Yeah," he said. "Things here have been a little off."

"Like what?"

"Well, you said that Dave mentioned some hokey stuff going on with the security, and so did she, but nobody really explained what it was."

"You really think it could be because of her?"

"If we look back since the accident, no matter what

we've done, the leads we've followed, getting answers has always led to other issues," Fallon said. "It's been one can of worms after another. So I wouldn't be surprised if that same thing isn't happening right now."

"Well, we can ask her."

"I wonder if she'd tell us," he said, with a twitch of his lips.

"Dave would."

"You're right. He would," Fallon said, as he pulled out his phone and quickly sent Dave a text. "The problem is, he's in the air and isn't likely to get this for a while."

"It's hard to say. It depends on how bad the signal quality is."

"From here, it'll be shitty. You know that."

"I know, but I was kind of hoping."

"Whenever we really need to get through to people, it rarely happens."

"I see she made you pie," Quinn said.

"She made *us* pie," he said, looking back at him in surprise.

"Uh-huh, you're the one who loves pie."

"You don't?"

"Well, I can't say I know anybody who doesn't love pie," he said. "But come on. She made it for you."

"No way," he said. "I'm calling bullshit on that one. You're not going to say it's all about me."

"No, of course not, but it's obvious that she would do anything for you."

"BS again," he said. "Don't even go there."

"You've already been there," he said. "Otherwise she wouldn't be so sensitive."

"Whatever," he said. Just then he leaned forward, closer

to the screen, and said, "So what's that right there?" He tapped the monitor.

"Was this last night?"

"I'm not sure," he said. They watched as the shadows shifted and moved and came up against one of the walls.

"Now that's interesting," he said. "Did they put something on the wall?"

"Maybe, but what would that device do?"

"It could just interfere or send signals on its own."

"I bet it interferes with our signals," he said. "Let's go take a look."

The two of them raced outside, and the new addition wasn't even well hidden. They stood and studied the small black box, attached just under one of the security cameras.

"It's not a professional job," Quinn suggested.

"No, it doesn't look it, does it?"

"So what does that mean then?"

"It means," Fallon said, "I'm thinking that we have another player in the mix. And I bet it has something to do with her."

They walked back inside to see her cutting the fresh pie, with ice cream off to the side.

"So we've got a couple questions for you," Quinn said.

She looked up, smiled, and said, "What do you want to know?"

"Has anybody around here been paying attention to you, that you would rather wasn't … paying you attention?"

She looked at Quinn and frowned, saying, "Are you asking me if I have a boyfriend?"

"No," Quinn said. "I'm very awkwardly trying to ask if anybody's giving you unwanted attention?"

Immediately a shutter came down over her eyes.

He shared a glance with Fallon, then nodded slowly. "You need to tell us."

"There's nothing to tell," she said. "Why?"

"Because it seems like there is something to tell, and it looks like whatever's going on with the security system could have to do with something other than Bullard."

"That makes no sense," she murmured, studying the two men in front of her.

"Yes," Quinn said. "So we need details. Now."

CHAPTER 3

"THERE'S NOTHING TO explain," Lindsey said. "If it was important, I'm sure Uncle Dave would have mentioned it to you."

"Well, that certainly gets our interest," Quinn said.

She shrugged. "Last time I was here, there was that guy—remember him?"

Quinn asked, "The delivery guy?"

"If that's the one you're talking about, that was a few years ago, wasn't it?" Fallon asked.

"Well, that's when it started, but he always seems to know when I come into town." She shrugged. "In the beginning, it was kind of flattering."

"And now it's obviously not," Fallon said, crossing his arms over his chest.

She could already see his anger vibrating, just at the edge of his frame. "No, it's not," she said. "But it hasn't gotten particularly bad either."

"Okay, so how bad has it gotten?" Quinn asked.

"He just won't take no for an answer."

"Well, that's bad enough," he said. "How far wrong has he gotten?"

"Come on," she said coolly. "It's not like he's attacked me or anything."

"How does he contact you?"

"He usually texts me or calls," she said. "Uncle Dave changed my number before I came over here, so the guy can't see if I'm in town. Because we were trying to figure out how he always knew when to call."

"Yeah, that's a good question. So how does he know?"

"Uncle Dave figured that he had some kind of alert set up, whenever I hit town."

"Well, that's fairly dedicated," Quinn said, sounding surprised. "Outside of keeping watch on the compound, I'm not sure how he'd do that."

"It's also fairly creepy," Fallon said. "Does Dave realize that something happened, since you came back?"

"Yes, but we thought we fixed it," she said. "I didn't think it had anything to do with the security system."

"Well, I don't like the sound of it either way," Fallon said, firming his jaw.

She stared at him. "It's got nothing to do with you anyway."

Quinn whistled at that. "Well, if that wasn't guaranteed to get his goat, I don't know what else would."

She glared at him. "It's got nothing to do with either of you. He's just some guy who's got it in his head that I'm supposed to be somebody special to him, and he's wrong."

"But some people get it in their head," Fallon said, "and unfortunately you've not shaken him loose, no matter what you tell him."

"So I'm supposed to just let this guy dominate my life or what?"

"Obviously we would have preferred that it not go down that way," Fallon said. "But a stalker like this can be very dangerous. And, if he's doing something to the security system, then that's even more dangerous."

"Do you know what he does for a living now?" Quinn asked.

"Last I knew, he was doing IT for a gold mine or something over here, working at one of the older mines," she said, with a shrug.

"An IT background is a little more concerning," Quinn said. "I think I'll take a walk around, take a closer look at that box he left behind, and see if we've got anything else happening."

"Sounds good," Fallon said. "Maybe take a bug detector too, to see if he's somehow gotten into the house."

"You think?" Quinn frowned. "I guess, with less of our team here, it's possible."

"In theory," Fallon said, "he could have shut down the security and come in at any point in time when he thought it was empty. Then he could have done whatever he wanted." Fallon turned and looked at her. "When did you get here?"

"Three days ago."

"When did he contact you last?"

"Within an hour of my arrival," she said in a dry tone. His eyebrows shot up, and she nodded. "I have no idea how he knew. Neither did Uncle Dave. He wasn't real happy about it, but he had a talk with the team, and they just laughed and said it wasn't any of them."

"But you had the guy's text."

"Uncle Dave gave him the warning of his life. The guy said somebody hacked his phone. Anyway, Uncle Dave didn't consider the guy much more than an overzealous admirer."

"He wasn't really worried about it?" She nodded. "So," Fallon continued, "if we told you that he had completely screwed with the electronics system so he could get in and out of the compound whenever he wanted, how would you feel?"

"A little more dismayed maybe," she said.

"I would hope so. The fact of the matter is, it looks like somebody has access to something we don't really want them to have access to, and that's a concern. Because, if he can get in and out, you could be sound asleep when he comes next."

In the end, Quinn jumped in and added, "Remember. He probably saw me leave with Dave."

She looked at him, chewed on her bottom lip, and she thought about it. "Do you think he's planning on coming in tonight?"

"I don't know what his plans are," Fallon said. "But I think it's something that we have to assume is possible and be prepared for it."

"In that case," she said, "maybe we shouldn't remove whatever he put in place and use it to trap him instead."

"I like the way she's thinking," Quinn said, with a big grin.

"But listen," she said. "You can't just assume that this guy is nothing more than a lovesick stalker because I haven't had any relationship with him."

"And that's possible," he said, "but it could also be exactly as it seems."

"I guess," she said. "It's still bizarre."

"No doubt about it," he said. "But that's how these stalkers can be. They get a very narrow focus, and nothing else is important in their world but getting the object of their desire."

"I really don't like the way you said that," she murmured.

"Maybe not, but maybe it'll keep you safer if it keeps

you more aware."

She shrugged. "Or you're just making too much out of it," she said lightly. But inside she knew that they weren't, and she realized this could be a serious problem. "Maybe I'll just go home early," she said, with a shrug.

"Well, you could, but then he'll just wait until you come back again."

"Once I go back, I could be there for years," she said.

"And yet you're so close to Dave. So, chances are, you'll come back and see him on a regular basis. Do you really want to deal with this every time?"

She sat here, tapping the counter, watching the ice cream melt. Finally she put away the ice cream and said, "You guys should eat." And she handed off the desserts.

"Do we get dinner first?"

"No," she said. "It's not dinnertime yet. And, hey, why wait?"

Neither of them argued, and they both quickly sat down and ate their pie in front of her.

She had a small piece, but her mind was consumed with the problems at hand. "I haven't had anything to do with him," she murmured. "I don't understand why he'd even care."

"You're a beautiful woman," Quinn said.

She looked up at him in surprise.

"When you're here, you're just part of the family," he said. "So you probably don't see yourself that way, but you are pretty amazing. So any other guy will see that and will be interested."

"So just because he wants it, he gets to have it, is that the idea?"

"Well, that's the problem. We hope it's not the idea, but

some guys think they can take whatever they want."

"Bastards," she said lightly.

"Yes, but it doesn't change the fact."

"Maybe not," she said. "But it doesn't exactly inspire confidence in the male species."

"You've never been short of admirers," Fallon said.

"Well, it's not like they're dropping at my feet either," she said. "I am too busy with my job and training to have much of a social life," she said. "So I don't really see why it's something I have to deal with now." The trouble was, it didn't matter what she felt; she had to deal with it. Because, chances were, it would be here right in her face. She shrugged. "Well, do what you guys can, and I'll just go home early."

With that, she got up and walked out.

"THAT WENT WELL," Quinn said.

"If you say so."

"I don't think avoidance is the way to handle it."

"No. Her stalker will just keep it up, going a little farther every time. He could even nab her at the airport or something. Imagine if Dave wasn't expecting her, and nobody else knows she's missing, until nobody hears from her for a while."

"I don't even want to think about that," Quinn said.

"No, but we see women kidnapped and held captive for years, all over the place. That's not what I would want for her."

"It's not what anybody would want for any woman," he muttered. "Such bastards that they even think they can do that."

"I know, so we have to find this guy and teach him a lesson," Fallon said.

"That's a good point, but how? It needs to be a big-enough lesson that he never comes back after her."

"That's not as easy as you'd think either. Kano put the fear of God into somebody on our last job, but that guy kept coming back, like a bad penny, and nearly beat his wife to death and threw her in a Dumpster," Fallon murmured.

"Some of them have to be sick in the head. I sure wouldn't want to piss off Kano. Some of these guys just don't know when to quit."

"Sometimes they're so afraid of the consequences of quitting that it's not in them to stop."

Quinn stared out in the distance. "I think she's right though, ... about setting a trap."

"In that case," he said, "we should do a reconnaissance and see what else there is."

"Then we'll check for bugs?"

"Crap, I got derailed with that whole conversation. Let's do a recon, then the bug check."

The two of them hopped up, and Fallon opened the oven to see a roast cooking inside. "Any idea when the roast will be ready?"

"No clue, but it's a little early for dinner, so I presume it'll be a while yet. Once it's dark out, no telling when the stalker will be back."

With that, they headed outside.

CHAPTER 4

UPSTAIRS, LINNY SAT on the side of her bed and stared out the window. The truth of the matter was, this guy had scared her for a long time now. She'd finally talked to her uncle about it, and he'd been horrified to think she'd been dealing with these kinds of issues. He promised her that, if he could do anything to stop it, he would, but even he hadn't picked up on how intense it was even now.

She had chalked that up to Uncle Dave's worry over Bullard because that dominated everything in their lives right now. And it was the scariest crap. To think that somebody could have gone after Bullard the way they had was insane, and she didn't believe that whatever was happening in her corner had something to do with that, but it was hard to not consider it at least. And that raised her fear level quite a bit. She wondered if she should ask the guys about it, though she'd been downplaying the whole topic for so long that it felt strange to let her fears come to the surface.

She realized it was time to deal with the roast anyway. She had packed up the measly bit of clothing she had brought with her and headed downstairs. It was already turning dark outside. In the kitchen she turned on the lights, pulled out the roast, put it onto a great big serving platter, and wrapped it up to keep it warm, while she checked on the veggies. Then she sent out a call on the intercom. "Dinner's in ten."

It had been at least two hours since they'd had pie. She was surprised at that. It seemed like the time had gone by so fast—too fast. There was never any end to it, but such was life. When she heard an odd sound behind her, she spun around but found nobody. The room was cool, empty, a storm gathering outside. She stared back out the window, feeling a creepiness wash over her. Just as she was about to call the men again, Fallon walked in. Though relieved to see him, she felt a sense of disquiet settling over her.

Fallon must have known somehow and walked over and grabbed her by her hands. "What's the matter?"

She shook her head and said, "I don't know. I just felt something was really wrong there for a moment." He tilted his head, and she shrugged, adding, "I don't really have a way to explain it. Maybe the storm outside had something scratching on the walls. It was just kind of creepy—but probably nothing."

"Maybe," he said, "but we also found bugs in two of the rooms."

She stared at him in shock. "What?"

"Yeah."

"What bugs? Where?"

"Quinn is still searching the command center, but one was in the big dining room and one in the offices."

"Which office?"

He sighed and said, "Dave's."

She said, "Well, that has nothing to do with my stalker guy, right?"

"I don't think so, but I don't know what's going on here. We've disabled both bugs and will trace any serial numbers we find on them," he said. "I texted Dave, but I don't think he's landed yet." Fallon checked the time and the schedule on his phone and said, "No, he's still in the air."

"Okay, that's a little disconcerting. How would somebody get a bug inside?"

"It wouldn't be all that hard, particularly if something was jamming the overall security system."

"But that just happened."

"Did you and Dave do anything since you've been here, like go out shopping or to dinner maybe?"

"No, but we've been out at the pool a lot," she said. "I needed to destress and relax."

"And that could be all that it took," he said. "Think about it. The pool's out back, and, if there was no security connection, there would be no alarms to hear. So somebody could have crept in and set up the bugs while you're out there."

She stared at him.

"What is it?" he asked.

"The day before yesterday," she said, "I asked Uncle Dave if somebody was in the house because I thought I heard something. He just laughed and said we were the only ones here."

"But he hasn't quite been himself either, has he?"

"No," she admitted. "He hasn't been, but he hasn't been off or weird or anything. Just distracted and stressed."

"No, I understand. Plus, he's been carrying a heavier load," he said.

"I don't like anything about this," she said, wrapping her arms around her chest. "Are you sure?"

"Are we sure we found bugs? Absolutely. Do we know who planted them? No, but we'll get this traced and figured out. Of course we don't think it's internal, meaning an inside job, but we have to consider it objectively, even though we don't want that to be true."

At that, her jaw opened, then slowly snapped shut. "Just please tell me that you don't think it's my uncle," she said, her emotions boiling to the surface.

He grabbed her by the shoulders and gave her a little shake, saying, "Hey, it's all right. I just said it's not Dave."

She took a deep breath and said, "Thank you. Of course it could be anybody else too, couldn't it?"

"It could be, but it's not likely."

"Too scary," she muttered.

"Yes, it is. Betrayal is always scary."

"*Betrayal*, that's such a hard word," she whispered.

"I don't know what other word to use," he said quietly.

She shrugged. "Oh, it's the right word. I just can't imagine anybody trying to cut down Bullard. He was always so full of life," she murmured.

"So does this guy who wants to date you, did he know Bullard?"

"I don't think so," she said, frowning. "Though I guess, since he's been in the area all this time, it's possible. But, honestly, if someone's around causing trouble, can we actually count on it being a separate issue from Bullard's death?"

"Bullard's *attack*, you mean?" he corrected. "No, but I'd like to have a little talk with this guy."

"Well, I have his number in my contacts. It was transferred with the rest when I got my new phone," she said, as she pulled it out, brought it up, and held it out for him.

He quickly took down the number and called it. When he got no answer, he said, "Let's see if we can trace it."

"What would that tell you?"

"Where he is right now." Fallon asked her, "So, with that IT work he does, does he travel much?"

"He said he had to do a bunch in the beginning but less now. It was more a case of when there were issues."

"Right," he muttered.

She watched as he headed to the command center with the number. "Don't you want dinner first?"

"I'll be there in a minute," he said, but she trailed behind him.

"What are you trying to do?"

"Just locate where he is right now."

"I'm pretty sure that's illegal," she muttered.

"All kinds of things in life are illegal," he said. "That includes killing our friends—or trying to kill our friends, I mean," he corrected. "However tracking a cell phone location is not."

She knew that he was working hard to keep Bullard alive in his mind, even against all the evidence or lack of evidence either way. It's just that the odds were against Bullard having survived at this point, and nobody wanted to deal with that. Still, she watched, as he sorted out some app system.

"Will that tell us if he's nearby?"

"It should tell us wherever he is, nearby or not, but I have to track it."

"Well, that's not necessarily an easy thing then, is it?" she muttered.

"Doesn't mean it's impossible though," he said. "A lot of people leave their phone on all the time." When nothing came back up on the screen, he shrugged and said, "I'll leave it set up, in case it gets turned on."

"Okay," she said. "Now will you eat?"

He chuckled. "Yep, come on. Let's go eat. And, with

that, he swung an arm around her shoulders, tucked her up close, and walked into the dining room.

Quinn looked up at them in surprise. She went to step away, but Fallon wasn't having it and held her close. As they got to the table, he motioned to one chair and said, "You can sit here."

"And what if I don't want to sit there?" she asked, feeling belligerent for whatever reason.

"Then please, pick a spot," he said and waved his hand at the entire expanse of the massive table. She shrugged and took the seat he had pointed out. She caught the smirk on his face as she did so, earning him a glare. She handed over the vegetables, as she took a little bit of meat and then passed it on.

"Smells good," Quinn said.

She smiled. "I learned to cook from Uncle Dave, so all these recipes are his."

"And it tastes fantastic," he muttered.

They quickly dug into the food in front of them, and she was more than happy to see how much they appreciated good food. It made such a difference between cooking for people who enjoyed food and cooking for people who just picked at it. But these men tucked in, like they hadn't had a meal in days. And maybe they hadn't; they'd been traveling so much.

Finally Fallon put down his fork and said, "That was really good."

"Thank you. It was, wasn't it?"

Just then a series of beeps came from the other room. Quinn looked up and asked, "What's that?"

But Fallon was already on his feet and racing that way. The two of them hopped up and joined him.

"What do you see?" she asked.

"It's picked up his phone," he said.

"Oh, good," she said. "So where is he? And can you tell who he's calling?"

"Well, that would be nice to know, wouldn't it?" he said, as he clicked a few more buttons. "It's not giving me the phone number called. I have to get into his phone records to see that."

"But where is he?"

Behind her, she heard Quinn gasp. She turned, while he stared at the map. "You guys can obviously figure this out, but I don't know what I'm looking at." Then she leaned closer. "Wait a minute," she said. "Isn't that local, here?"

"Not only is it local," Quinn said, "but it's like seriously local. As in, the guy is here, and I think he's literally right outside the compound."

She stared at him, shook her head, and said, "That's not possible."

"Why not?"

"He told me that he wasn't in town."

"Well," Fallon said, "wasn't that two or three days ago? And didn't you tell me that you'd heard a noise that day you and Dave were out by the pool? Guess what? He's in town now. Plus, he's probably a lying bastard anyway."

She couldn't believe it. It was just too much, and she hadn't even gotten a thought fully processed before the men raced toward the front door. She called out, "Wait! Shouldn't we at least be armed?"

Fallon called back, "We are. You stay inside."

She frowned at that and followed them to the front door, stepping just outside. She had no clue what was going on, but a gate was on the far side of the fence. Was this guy actually here at the gate, or was he somewhere else? It was just too hard to tell. As she stood on the front porch, both men searched the grounds. She didn't think this guy could have gotten that far into the compound, but she knew saying anything wouldn't do any good. The guys were on a mission, and that was beyond something she could stop or slow down. Yet, as she watched, the two men looked at each other and approached the big gates.

Twin heavy wrought-iron gates barred the entrance, but it was hard to see clearly through with that much iron involved. They went to the small side gate, both crouching, as if looking for an enemy on the other side. She stood here, wondering and watching. When the men returned a moment later, their faces were grim. She raised both hands and said, "Well?"

"Get back in the house," Fallon snapped.

"I'm not some little woman to be ordered around," she said coolly.

"No," he said. "But a murdered man, connected to you, is outside the front gate."

She stared at him in shock. "Murdered?"

Quinn nodded, as he walked toward her. Fallon had already headed toward the small gate again.

"I don't understand," she said faintly.

"What's to understand? The reason we could pick him up with the trace was because his phone was left on. And he was right outside, as we thought. Literally just outside the gate."

She stared at him. "But I thought *he* was the danger."

"The game has changed," he said, his voice hard.

She stared at Quinn, still trying to process this. "Are you saying that somebody murdered him, just like that?"

"But we don't know whether he was murdered because somebody thought he was part of this team," he muttered, "or he was murdered because he'd served his usefulness or he was murdered because he was involved in something else completely unrelated."

She blinked, struggling to absorb everything he'd just told her, but it seemed so unbelievable. "Let me see him," she said.

He shook his head.

She glared and put her hands on her hips. "I can at least identify him." Quinn frowned at that, and she nodded. "Yeah, let's make sure that we have the right guy at least." At that, she turned and stormed toward the front gate.

Quinn called out, "Fallon, we're coming to you."

"Are you sure?"

"Yeah, she wants to ID him."

"If you say so." They came through the side gate, headed to the main gates, and found Fallon sitting there. He had covered the face and part of the deceased's body with his jacket. At her nod, he lifted it up.

She stared down at the young man in shock. "It's him," she said faintly. "I don't understand. Why would Ben even be here?" she asked Fallon.

"Nobody'll understand why now, what with him dead and all."

Quinn looked at Fallon. "I could call the local cops but—"

"I know. I think we should bring him inside and instead call a few of our network groups."

"Bullard and Kasha used to handle all that," Quinn stated.

"I know who to call," she said. She didn't even need to

check the body further because it was obvious he was dead—half of his head had been blown away. She looked at the body again and asked, "So what kind of weapon would have done that?"

"Several, but nothing small," Fallon said. "The damage to the side of his head is pretty extensive."

"So are we looking at a long-range weapon?" she asked, motioning around. "Because nothing suspicious is here."

"I would highly suspect," Fallon continued, "based on the lack of blood pooling around the body, that he was killed elsewhere and dropped here."

She nodded. "And that would make sense. I don't do the forensic stuff that you guys talk about. I work more on the side of saving people, not killing them."

"Well, we didn't kill this guy. Remember?"

She nodded slowly. "So why is he dead?"

"Quite likely his association with you." She felt the ground shift under her feet. Fallon reached out a hand and said, "I don't mean that you're to blame."

She looked up at him, then frowned and said, "But, in a way I am, aren't I?"

"No," Fallon said with added emphasis. "Don't even go there."

"Hard not to," she whispered, rubbing her forehead.

"No," he said. "This is not part of it."

"How can it not be?" she cried out.

"Calm down," Quinn said, as he looked at Fallon. "I suggest we completely remove the evidence, if you don't think anybody's coming for the body."

"No, wait," she said, pulling out her phone. "Uncle Dave gave me some numbers." She quickly hit Dial on one. "Hi," she said. "Uncle Dave gave me this number."

The man on the other end said, "Yes. What can I do for you?"

"A man's outside the gate," she said boldly. "And he's dead."

"Right. You're the doctor, aren't you?"

"Yes," she said, with a small smile. "A lot of good it's doing right now."

"That compound tends to end up with more cases of death than injury anyway," he said. "I'm on my way."

She tucked the phone in her pocket and said, "Okay, he's coming."

"Who is?" Quinn asked.

She pulled out her phone again, checked the name on her Contacts, and said, "All Uncle Dave put down is *Wagner the Fixer.*"

At that, Fallon smiled. "Good guy to call," he said.

"You didn't really call the cops, did you?" Linny asked Quinn.

"Not in this case, no," Quinn said. "They aren't exactly the people we want to deal with right now."

"But we didn't kill him," she protested.

"Very true, but the law out here is a little bit rogue—on its own."

"I thought that's how it was at the other compound," she muttered. She frowned, as she looked at the body again. "Any other injuries?"

"Haven't looked yet," Fallon said, but, crouched beside the body, he inspected Ben's arms, hands. "I'm not seeing any signs of torture or indication of being tied up."

"Right," she said. "I was thinking of that too. None that I can see." She studied Ben for a long moment and said, "No, I don't see anything else. Check his ID."

"I already have," Quinn said. "His driver's license is here. Ben Radcliffe. He has no credit cards, no cash and no phone. So they've destroyed that somehow or we wouldn't have found him."

"So they killed him and robbed him blind too?"

"I wouldn't be at all surprised," Quinn said.

"Why would they leave anything to identify him?" she asked, frowning. "Right back to the cloak-and-dagger stuff."

"It's the life. Remember?"

She acknowledged that slowly. "I do." Then she shut her mouth at that point because she really did understand. She'd been here too much in her life, not that she was ever involved like this, but it wasn't like Uncle Dave to hide any of it from her. How do you hide something like that, when her own parents had been murdered? "So now what?"

"We wait for Wagner," Fallon said. "And consider this scenario further. There's not much blood, for one."

"And is Wagner likely to take away the body? In this heat, it won't be long before it gets riper."

"Well, that's one of the other questions. How long do we think he's been dead?"

"There's blood but not fresh," she said. "So I would say he's probably been dead at least ten or twelve hours."

"So his killer kept him where? He's plenty ripe already."

She frowned at that. "It's not exactly a clear answer, is it?"

"Nope, sure isn't, but welcome to the world of the puzzles we live in."

She frowned at that and then bent to check his wrist temperature. "It's hard to say if he was even in a cooler. But, if he was dead for half a day," she said, "I would have expected a lot more decomposition in this heat. So a fridge is a good answer potentially."

"I agree with that assessment," Fallon said, studying the body. "Nothing here differentiates him. No different clothing—nothing. What we've got is a white Caucasian male, and his ID has him identified as Ben Radcliffe, thirty years old. But, other than that, we don't have anything to go on."

"Which means what?" Lindsey asked.

"Means we need to do a full workup on his life," Fallon said.

"That seems almost insulting," she said.

"Maybe, but he isn't worried about it now, is he?"

"But that doesn't mean we have to be so intrusive."

"We have to find out who killed him in order to find out what message they were trying to send us."

"Isn't that obvious?" she said, pointing at the dead body. "It's a warning."

"It is, indeed," Quinn said, with an approving nod, "but it's also a threat."

"Meaning?"

"Meaning, you're next," Fallon said.

"And did you mean that, as in, *I'm* next?" she asked. "Or did you mean that, as in, one of us is next?"

"I highly suspect it's both," he said.

"We're back to that Bullard thing, right?"

"Yes, with the possibility that this guy was in the wrong place at the wrong time or was just a patsy for this killer to use."

"Who uses another person to send a message?"

"Killers all over the world do," Quinn said.

Just then a vehicle drove down the road. As it came closer, Quinn took a few steps toward it and waited until it slowed. When Wagner hopped out, a man that he knew well, Quinn reached out and shook his hand. "Glad to see you."

"I'm surprised you called me," Wagner said.

"I didn't," he said. "Linny here did."

He looked at Linny and said, "Dave's niece, right?"

"Yes." She walked forward and shook his hand. "These guys were quite prepared to take him out back and bury him," she said. "But I was afraid there might be a family looking for answers."

At her words Fallon gave a short bark of laughter.

Wagner just looked at him sideways and said, "She's telling the truth. Admit it."

He shrugged and said, "He has to be deposited somewhere, before he gets any riper."

"Yeah," Wagner said, with a nod. "I brought a body bag." He shook it out, readying it for transport.

"Good." And, with that, the three guys quickly lifted Ben into the body bag.

"What will you do with him?" Linny asked.

"Take him back to the morgue," Wagner said.

"You'll do a full forensic workup?" she asked.

"I'll do that right away," he said. "I already looked at the satellite feeds, found somebody heading down this driveway."

"Right," Fallon said. "Did you happen to see him drop off the body?"

"Looked like he had a passenger, sleeping against the window. No blood is here," he added. "And we already have the transport vehicle."

That startled Fallon, who looked at Wagner and said, "What?"

Wagner nodded. "If you had kept on going down the road, you'd have seen the vehicle. It's got a little bit of blood in the back end. So he came down here, dumped off the body, then went back there to dump the vehicle. There was a phone tossed on the seat. Presumably it belonged to your dead guy that you tracked here. Only the SIM card is missing and it's been damaged."

"Interesting tactic," Quinn said.

"Yeah, the problem is, it's exactly that—a tactic." He turned to Fallon. "So what does this guy want?"

"It could be the death of the team, for all we know," Fallon said. "It's hard to say."

"No news on Bullard yet?" Wagner asked. Both men shook their heads. Wagner looked at Linny. She shrugged and said, "They're all still hoping for a miracle."

"Well, if there ever was a miracle to be had, it would be Bullard who would put it into play," he said.

Just then another vehicle came in behind his.

"And here's the coroner," Wagner said.

"I thought you would load him up and take him with you," she exclaimed.

"Nah," he said. "I'm doing it officially, just in case it's all connected to Bullard's death. So who was this guy anyway?"

"You should ask her that," Fallon said. "An admirer."

Wagner looked at her in surprise.

She glared at Fallon. "Not quite."

"Well, what else would you call it?" he asked.

She looked at Wagner. "A stalker. Some guy who wouldn't take no for an answer. Uncle Dave had a talk with him because he was getting very arrogant."

"Interesting, of course, with Dave not being here—"

"He flew out today."

"And Quinn and I came in this morning," Fallon said. "So maybe Ben didn't realize that."

"It's an easy mistake to make," Wagner said.

"Not really." Fallon laughed. "Why would they have not assumed Quinn came back from dropping off Dave at the airport?"

"He must have missed it," Wagner said. "Or maybe he didn't see the vehicle. I don't know."

"No, we don't know." Quinn nodded. "I agree absolutely."

"Will you tell Dave?" Wagner asked the group.

"Absolutely," Fallon said, "but he's not landed yet."

"Fine." The body was loaded up, and the forensics team went to work on the ground, looking for evidence, but it didn't take long. They had the drop-off vehicle already, so trying to track anything about the vehicle could wait. Now it was more about footprints. As they looked, it was easy to see that a rake had been used back to where the car had been abandoned.

"And the rake was used at the other end too?" Fallon asked.

"Absolutely," Wagner said. "So we already have a good idea what we're looking at."

"Sucks," Quinn noted.

"It does," Wagner said. "But what else is new? You guys never ever give us easy cases to work on."

"No, because you'd get too complacent then," Fallon said, and, with that, they headed back, leaving Wagner and his men to their job.

Once inside the compound again, she looked around and said, "I'll head to bed."

"Are you sure you're okay?" Fallon asked.

She gave a half laugh. "Sure, I'm just fine," she said. "It happens all the time, right?"

"It shouldn't happen at all," he said quietly, his gaze intent on her face.

She frowned at him. "I'm fine."

He nodded. "You're still leaving?"

"I don't know what I'm doing," she said, sagging into the closest seat, which happened to be one of the stools by the kitchen island.

"I suggest you stay," Quinn said.

She looked at him, surprised. "That's not what I expected you to say."

"No, but, until we really know what's going on," he said, "I don't know how safe you are."

"Because you think this is connected to me somehow. Is that it?"

"We can't be sure that it *isn't* connected to you," Fallon said. "So we can't brush this off as being not connected, and, until that can be confirmed, we have to assume that it is."

"We don't know this man Ben. You do," Quinn said.

She frowned at the logic, placed her elbows on the island, dropping her forehead into her hands. "And I don't have much of a connection with him," she muttered.

"Not much is still more than none."

"I know," she said, and she did know. It just wasn't anything she wanted to deal with. "I'm staying the night," she said. "Then I'll see how I feel in the morning." With that, she got up and walked out and headed to her room.

QUINN AND FALLON looked at each other. Fallon said, "Well, we know what needs to be done now."

Quinn nodded. "Let's go take this kid's life apart."

And that's what they did. It took hours, and, by the time Fallon lifted his head from the focused work he had been doing, he still didn't have a hell of a lot on his plate to show for it. He looked back at Quinn to see him still buried in documents as well. Just then Fallon's phone rang; it was Dave. "Are you okay, Dave?" Fallon put the call on Speaker.

"Yeah, I'm okay but stuck in transit," he said. "We had some plane trouble, and they're working on it right now. They kept us on the plane for the longest time, and we had no reception. Now I'm off to the little airport for a few minutes. I've been trying to call. My instincts were screaming at me. What the hell's going on at home?"

At that, Fallon's eyebrow shot up. "Yeah, well, we've had a little bit of trouble, but nothing to worry about."

"Let me be the judge of that," he said. "What's going on?"

Fallon explained, "Remember that kid, Ben, the one who wouldn't take no for an answer with Linny?"

"Hell yes. That guy was a pain in the ass. Make sure you convince him not to come around anymore," he snapped. "That kid's just bad news."

"Well, I don't imagine he's a kid, and the truth of the matter is that he's dead." He quickly filled him in on what happened.

"Jesus, Fallon," he said. "You're not even home five minutes, and we've got dead bodies everywhere."

"Hardly everywhere, and it's not like I even killed him," Fallon said, his tone dry.

"Maybe not," he said. "It's like all this shit follows you around."

"I didn't do anything," he protested.

"Well, now you better tear apart Ben's life and see what the hell's going on."

"Oh, don't worry," he said. "We are."

"Better yet," Dave said, "I'm coming home."

"No, you're not."

"Yes, I am," Dave said, warming to the idea. "That's got to be why this plane and everything else didn't let me go forward anyway," he said. "I'm telling you that it's a sign."

"Screw that idea," he said. "Somebody needs to see if Bullard is one of those men."

"It'll be a waste of my time," he said.

"Well, we're looking after your niece," he said. "So don't insult us by saying we can't do the job."

At that, Dave hesitated.

"Look, Dave. I know. She's the only family you've got. We get it. And we're looking after her. And, if you want to come home, come home, but don't do it on the assumption that you can do a better job than we can."

"It's not that," he said. "I just don't want anything to happen to her."

"We get that," he said. "We also get the fact that you're almost there. Check out those men, and then, if you want to turn around and come back, that's a different story."

At that, Fallon felt the wheels turning, and Dave finally said, "Fine. Don't let anything happen to her."

Fallon realized that, for Dave, this really would be the be-all and end-all for him.

"We won't," he said gently.

"Even better, lock her up," he said cheerfully. "Just keep her completely locked down, so that nobody can get in or go out."

"Well, wouldn't that be nice? Except she's already talking about leaving … tomorrow."

"She was supposed to be there for a lot longer than that," he said. "That's one of the reasons I went on this trip. I wasn't even going to go, but she promised she'd stay."

"Well, I'm glad to hear that," Fallon said, "because now I can use it to keep her here."

"I want her there when I get home, Fallon. She's got over a month off."

"Oh, in that case," he said, "we'll definitely keep her here. I thought she only had a few days off."

"No," Dave snapped. "She better be there when I get home. Hey, they're calling my flight. I have to go." With that, Dave hung up.

Quinn stared at Fallon in surprise. "She's got all that time off?"

"Yeah, so why the hell the quick exit?" Fallon wanted to know.

Quinn shook his head. "Hard to know."

"*I* know," Fallon said. "It's probably me."

"You don't know that," Quinn said.

"Hell yeah, I do. She's always been like that."

"No, you mean *you've* always been like that."

Fallon looked at his buddy in surprise. "What? I didn't do anything."

He chuckled. "Exactly," he said. "That's the problem. You won't make that step, so it's probably a case of her needing to run away."

"Does she look like the type to run anywhere?"

"No, she sure doesn't," he said, "but you know what I mean."

"I think you're wrong," Fallon said.

"And I think you're wrong," he said.

"Fine, we'll agree to disagree. Again."

"We've done it plenty of times before."

"Doesn't change the fact that you're still wrong." Fallon glared at his friend.

But Quinn just chuckled and said, "You find anything?"

"No, outside of his fixation with her, there's nothing."

"Well, the fixation makes sense. She's beautiful. She's talented. I won't say she's superwealthy, but she definitely has huge career potential, and she's well connected to this compound."

"That's not a plus for a lot of people." Fallon chuckled.

"No, it sure isn't, not right now especially."

"So where does this leave us?"

"Digging deeper, I guess," Quinn said.

"I want his friends and associates and anybody he worked with," Fallon stated. "Somebody knew that he had a connection here."

"So now we look at social media?" Quinn suggested. "Or chat rooms? Maybe he belonged to a group? Just too many possible forums to search out, don't you think?"

"The trouble is," Fallon said, "not only are there too many forums but too many aliases he could have used at any time. So we'd just be looking for a needle in a haystack. And we don't have time to spare for that shit. We need to check out the guy's apartment, see if we can find anything, like a laptop." Fallon glanced at his watch, looked at Quinn, and said, "Well, one of us has to stay here."

"And that's you," Quinn said, hopping to his feet. "Besides, I slept all the way here."

"You're not going alone," he said.

"You got another idea?"

"Yes," she said in the doorway. "Let's all go."

Fallon turned to see Linny, wearing a pajama top and short-short PJ bottoms covered by a loose robe, as she glared at him. "You're supposed to be asleep."

"I would have been, but I heard you talking to Uncle Dave after the phone beeped. And I figured it was something important for him to have called at this hour."

"He was just calling in response to the message I left earlier," he said.

She nodded. "Says you. So what's the verdict?"

CHAPTER 5

L INNY REALLY HAD been sound asleep, but her bladder had woken her up, and, when she'd heard the phone, curiosity had gotten the better of her. She stared at the two men, as they looked at each other, then back at her. "I also heard you tell him that you would look after me, so obviously he won't be happy if you two go off and leave me alone."

"Which we would never do," Fallon said, jumping to his feet.

"Right, yet you need to go investigate this guy's apartment, as I understand it. Correct?"

"We haven't found anything on our first round of digital research," Quinn said, with a nod. "So the next logical step would be to check his online presence, which is much easier to do if we have his laptop or phone or some electronic device that he used. Did you have any contact with him online?"

"No, I met him at the airport a long time ago."

"Right, so only contact in person and via text, correct?"

"Yes, and we found no phone on his body, so why would you think a laptop would be at his place?"

"We don't know, but it would cut out a lot of assumptions if we could go look, and it could really speed up the process if a quick trip would tell us something. Besides, everyone has electronics these days."

She frowned, nodded, and said, "I'll go get changed."

"No," he said. "I promised Dave that I'd keep you here and safe."

"You can promise Uncle Dave all the hell you want," she snapped. "You won't change my mind." Fallon looked at Quinn, and she shrugged and said, "Go ahead and tell Uncle Dave that. He already knows. He's just hoping that you'll have more influence over me than he would."

"Will you be this difficult all the time?" Fallon asked.

She gave him a bright smile. "If you'll be difficult with me, yes." With that, she disappeared, racing upstairs to get changed. By the time she was dressed and back down again, the men waited in the front hallway. "That's smart," she said.

Fallon just raised an eyebrow. She smiled and didn't say anything. "Smart in that we waited for you?"

"Well, you wouldn't leave anybody alone," she said. "So this was smart, and we'll go as a unit."

"It's still not smart. A man was killed over this connection to you. Have you forgotten?"

"I live with death every day. Remember?" she said in no uncertain terms. "What I hate is senseless death. And that's what this is."

"Got it," he muttered. Once in the garage, they headed to the large SUV.

"Why this one?"

"Bulletproof glass," Quinn said, as he slid into the driver's seat.

She raised her eyebrows at Fallon, but he just motioned her toward the back seat. "In you get."

She didn't argue because she knew she was already pushing it, just by the fact that she was here in the first place. She knew it was the right thing to do, but that didn't mean they were willing to agree. If she knew one thing, it was that all these men were tough asses and rarely gave in. So she would take her victory where she could enjoy it.

As soon as they pulled out onto the main road, and the big gates had closed behind them, she said, "I wonder why this compound is here?"

"Bullard's had it for a long time," Fallon said. "The city's been growing up all around him."

"Well, we're a good twenty minutes from the city," she said. "But still, you'd think that this area would be even more deserted."

"A lot of people work here. A lot bring in supplies. I think, just as the world changed and grew, this area became more populated."

"It's too bad though," she said. "A little more distance from it all would be nice."

"It certainly would," Fallon said. "Not so easy to do though."

"No," she said, then stayed quiet, as she watched where they traveled. "Did you hear anything from Wagner?"

"Nope. He hasn't responded or offered any information yet."

"Is he likely to?"

"Nope, I don't think so," Quinn said. "Why would he? He says what he has to, in order to deal with us, but other than that, it's a no-go."

"But he's the one Uncle Dave always told me to contact," she protested.

"Yes, with the understanding that everybody here plays their own game," he said.

She settled back, wishing that weren't so. At least in

America, the justice system was delineated, written down somewhere. But here? It was a whole lot different. She hated that. She understood it gave Bullard and his team more leeway for the work that they had to do, and a pretense of justice was involved along the way, but it wasn't as clear-cut, and it was a whole lot easier to deviate when they needed to.

"Any reason you're staying in America for your studies?" Quinn asked.

"It's where the best opportunities have presented themselves," she admitted. "Plus, I still need to do some more specialty work, and the bulk of my training opportunities are there."

He nodded.

"When you're done," Fallon asked, "where will you work?"

"Probably in the US," she said. "I like coming here to visit, but I'm not sure it's the place I want to stay."

"They need your help here."

"A lot of people need my help," she muttered. "Also that's an argument Uncle Dave's used on me many times, so don't bother."

"He just wants to have you nearby, so he can see you more, that's all."

"That makes sense, but—"

"Did Bullard set you on the path for surgery?"

"He does so much of it already," she said. "The stuff that I already knew before I ever got to med school put me miles ahead of the others."

"Except for the drug interactions, correct?"

"And that's mostly because he hasn't kept up with some of the more cosmetic drugs," she said.

"So being here with him hasn't been all that bad then,"

Fallon noted.

She looked at him in surprise. "It's been great," she said. "Seriously it's because of what I saw here, and the people we were helping all the time, that got me interested in med school in the first place."

"You might want to consider that Bullard, if he's alive, won't necessarily be capable of keeping up the same schedule."

She was silent for a moment. "I know," she answered, but she didn't want to discuss it further. That very notion had been in the back of her mind for a long time, but, if she was over in the US—and happy doing what she was doing— it was easier to forget about the people who needed so much more than the Western world had available for its own people. Kindly, as if understanding that this was still a conflict for her, the men fell silent.

As they drove closer and closer to the GPS bubble she saw on their tracker, she asked, "Is this the only reason we're going? Looking for electronics, I mean?"

"We're looking for anything important," Quinn said. "And we won't really know it until we see it."

"Right," she said. "So, for the moment, we'll assume everything is important?"

"Exactly."

THE TRIO PULLED around the corner from the address that they wanted. Fallon looked at her and said, "I suppose there's no point in asking you to wait here."

"Will I be safer here than with you?" At his frown, she smiled and said, "No, of course I won't be. Therefore, I'm coming with you."

"Why are you all of a sudden worried about your safety?"

"Okay, so I'm coming," she said cheerfully. "But now I'm not above using it to get what I want." And, with that, she hopped out with a trill of a laugh that echoed musically in the silence around them. Even Quinn grinned like a fool when he got out.

Fallon frowned at them. "You're both nuts."

"Nutty as can be," she said, with a nod. "Lead the way."

He shook his head and headed toward the address, checking the area as they approached. But it was as dead as it was quiet, except for rustling sounds and birdsong, so it's not like there would be any early warning that something awful was going on. He looked at Quinn and said, "Looks clear."

"It is, yes." He was on his phone, tracking something though.

"What are you looking at?" Linny asked Quinn.

"It's not so much that I'm looking at anything," he said. "I'm just doing a check around to make sure we're not looking at any problems coming from other vehicles."

They headed to the main entrance to the apartments, one where you had to ring to get access to.

"So," Quinn noted, "he had money for something like this."

"Sure," she said, "but it's not like it was much." They punched in the number for his apartment and, of course, got no answer on the other end. It was also dark outside, and nobody was likely to open up the front door for them, since they didn't know them.

He looked at her and frowned. "Look away," Fallon said.

"I'm not watching you," she answered. "Do what you need to do."

At that, he glanced at Quinn, then stepped forward and quickly disarmed the door. It was a little more complicated because it was an older system than he was used to. By the time he was done, she was watching over his shoulder with interest. He just rolled his eyes at her.

"Took you longer than I expected."

He glared at her, but she smiled, patted his cheek, and walked past him into the hallway. And again Quinn was grinning.

"It was an older system," Fallon said. "I haven't done one of those in a while."

"Of course," she said, as if that was completely normal and acceptable.

But Fallon also realized that he was thinking about showing off for her, and that just pissed him off all the more. With Quinn still acting like everything was fine—basically they were all having a grand old time—Fallon stormed ahead and up to the apartment. They had to walk up to the fourth floor. He didn't want to be stuck in an elevator, in case anybody found out that they were where they shouldn't be. The apartment was at the farthest end.

When they found the door in question, it was ajar. He motioned toward the open door, and both he and Quinn took up positions on either side, pulling their weapons. With Quinn going high and Fallon going low, they entered the apartment looking for anybody or anything. But it was empty. Deserted. And completely tossed. With her stepping in behind them, Fallon quickly closed the door, using his boot to close it completely. He pulled gloves from his pocket and handed two to Quinn, then two more to Linny.

"Don't touch anything," he cautioned.

"So why the gloves then?" she asked curiously.

"In case you forget."

She shrugged. "Well, it's definitely something I'm used to anyway." She pulled on the gloves with a *snap* and wandered around the small space. "It's hard to imagine the guy I knew living here," she said.

At that, the two men stopped, looked at her, and asked, "What do you mean?"

"It's just he looked so neat and tidy."

"But his place has been trashed—he didn't do this," they said.

She nodded. "I thought he would have had a higher-end place."

"Did he look like he had money?"

"I'm not sure that he did or he didn't," she said, "but he gave the impression of being a little more upper class."

"Well, a white South African isn't guaranteed a position of wealth," he said. "But there is more of a chance than not of being one of the wealthier families."

"I don't think he necessarily fit into that classification either," she muttered, and she wandered the small space.

"Stay here with us, please," Fallon called out.

She had found the doorway to the bedroom. "What difference does it make?"

He just stared at her, until she shrugged and came back toward him.

"Fine," she said, then waited for him while he searched through the place. "Like you said, the laptop is what we need. Do we have no sign of that?"

"Once the place was tossed, the odds of finding that became pretty slim," he said. When a knock came on the door, they froze.

A woman's voice called out, "Ben, you in there?"

With his finger to his lips, Fallon held the warning signal up for her to be quiet. She just raised an eyebrow, and he glared at her.

"Hey, I just want to say I'm sorry, if you're in there. I know I wasn't very nice last time. And, well, when I heard you come in, I just thought it would give me a chance to apologize again. We'll talk tomorrow." She said everything in an apologetic tone of voice, and they heard her footsteps going down the hallway.

At that, Fallon whispered, "Did you recognize her voice?"

She shook her head immediately. "I really don't know anything about his life," she said apologetically.

He nodded. "Well, that might be a good thing." As he walked into the bedroom, he stopped and stared. "Unless you're into all this kind of stuff."

She stepped up behind him and gasped. "Wow." The place was full of sex toys of various shapes and sizes. "Why are they out on display like that?"

"Where would you expect them to be?" he asked.

"I'd expect them to be in a drawer or a closet," she said. "This isn't normal for me."

"Good," he said. "But it does bring up an interesting aspect to his personality."

"Why would he think I'd be up for all this?"

"Because of that," Fallon said, as he stepped into the bedroom. She turned to look and behind him, on the back of the bedroom door, were pictures of her: pictures of her walking, getting off the airplane, and driving. A lot of them.

"Oh, my God," she gasped. "That's seriously creepy."

"Well, it does tell us that he's been watching you a whole lot more than you thought."

"A whole lot more," she said, shaking her head. "I had no idea this was going on."

"Stalkers rarely show their hand, until they get a little bit more active than we like to see them," he muttered. "It's an interesting thing though."

"No, it isn't," she snapped. "Nothing's interesting about it. *Interesting* is like, something I want to learn more about, something that's intriguing, something that looks fun. This is creepy and terrifying. Definitely not *interesting*."

"Well, it might help explain why he ended up outside the gate though."

"How the hell does him being a creeper explain how he ended up outside my gate?"

"Maybe somebody thought they were doing you a favor or doing Dave a favor," Fallon said, turning to look at Quinn.

"We need to talk to Dave again."

"I know. All kinds of information is here on you, Linny. He's pulled your DMV records, and he's even got your New York address."

"What?" she said, stepping up beside him.

He tapped the photo with his gloved finger. "See? It's got the school you went to."

"And yet some of this is pretty old," she said, staring. "That was my old address. Not my current address."

"No?"

"No," she said. "I moved about six weeks ago."

"Why?"

"I was just trying to get closer to work," she said. "Nothing is special about any of the places where I live. Basically just beds for me to drop into."

"So you moved so you could get closer?"

"I don't like commuting, if I don't have to," she said. "So I just chose to move to a smaller apartment."

"Six weeks you said, so he's not very far behind you then?"

"Well, I wasn't in this place in the photo all that long either," she admitted. "Maybe six months."

"Still, that's pretty creepy."

She shut the bedroom door, facing all the photos there. "I don't like the thought of him having any of this information on me. Can't we just rip it off of there?"

"Not yet," he said.

"But what if somebody else knows about it? What if somebody else thought this was a good idea?"

"Well, that's possible," he said, "and something I've been wondering."

"What? So you have another creeper who thinks like this guy? I don't think it works that way."

"It may or may not," he said, opening the bedroom door to take her focus off the photos on the backside. "The problem is, we don't have enough information."

She rolled her eyes at that. "You won't get anything from here either."

"Not so sure about that," he said, as he walked to the night table, which was tossed upside down, the contents of the drawers scattered about. "We need some idea of how this guy found you and how he operated. Was he alone? Did he have friends? Was he in a chat room? Did he have a little black book of other women?" At that, he straightened, turned, looked at the front door, and said, "What about his neighbors?"

"I got this one," Quinn said, and he walked to the door and stepped out of the apartment.

When the door closed quietly behind him, Fallon looked at her and said, "You never saw him with anybody?"

"No," she said. "I never saw him at all, other than that first time in the airport. I just talked to him a couple times. That's why his pushiness seemed really off."

"Well, it was," he said, "and it's not your fault. Remember that."

"He's still dead," she snapped. Then she stopped and slowly rotated her neck. "*Ugh.* I'm letting it get to me," she muttered. "I'm sorry."

"You're entitled. Somebody you know is dead," he muttered quietly. "That's upsetting, whether you liked him or not. And, no matter how much you deal with death on a regular basis, it's still a bit of a shock when it hits this close to home."

"It is," she said, "but I didn't know this guy at all, so I don't have any way to help you."

"No." He bent down and picked up a book. "*Kamasutra*," he read out loud. He opened it up and out slipped a folded piece of paper with a phone number. He held it out to Linny. "This is from your school. He's got your number."

"But I didn't give it to him," she stated, looking at the piece of paper. "They're not allowed to give out personal information."

"Maybe not, but all of us, at various times in our lives, have provided information that we're not supposed to. People will listen to a story and will be susceptible to something that might have been said. So, even though it's not their policy, it looks like somebody may have crossed a line, and you have no way of knowing who."

"I suppose if Ben said he was my brother or something."

"Exactly."

"So he had my number. So what?" she said. "He had it before. That's why Uncle Dave changed it. It doesn't tell us anything."

"No, and that's kind of interesting too. Why doesn't it tell us what we need to know? Because there's no laptop. Nothing's here." He walked back to the pictures of her on the door and carefully lifted one of them. "*Huh,*" he said. "Look at this. Written on the back of the picture is Sent to Peter, then an email address. Look. This one says, Sent to John. Same thing."

She stared at him, walked back over, and said, "Are you telling me that he's emailing these photos out?"

"Looks like it," he said. "The question is, was he doing it for money, or was he doing it for fun? Were these friends, or were these people part of the same group? And were they all stalking you, or was he stalking you for somebody else?"

She stared at him and started to shake. "I don't know," she said. "Please find out."

He quickly took out his phone, taking pictures of her photos on that door. He wanted all the details he could possibly get. As they flipped over each photo, each one had a different message, several of them were sent to the same men. "So there's four of them," he muttered.

"Yet I don't know any of them," she murmured.

"Yep," he said. "We've got emails, so that's something."

"But not enough."

"Take a look around, and see if you can see any notations about websites, forums, or names," he said. "Scrap pieces of paper seem to be this guy's thing."

"And how completely disorganized is that," she muttered.

"Doesn't particularly matter," he said, "because what

we're really after are the details here."

"Right," she said and quickly lifted and sorted through various bits and pieces in the living room. "I'm not seeing very much," she muttered.

"Keep looking." He then quickly added, "Wait, hang on. Come back here." She stopped looking and went to the bedroom again and saw that he was still at the door, taking pictures. "Do you know a Talbot? A Keith Talbot?"

"No, I don't know the name," she said. "I don't think I know anybody named Keith."

"Interesting," he murmured. "He's here a couple times."

"I wonder if he's local?"

"It's possible, but, in a digital age, he could be anywhere."

"So how do we contact this guy?"

"We'll start a search when we get home," he muttered. "I finally have a copy of everything. Let's check the insides of all closets and cabinets and everywhere else to make sure we haven't missed anything else."

"The other question is," she began, "who else would have searched this place?"

"Well, the cops should have been here," Fallon said. "They have Ben's dead body, so the authorities should be looking into his life, also his apartment."

"But they didn't do this." She swung her arms wide at all the mess in here.

"Not legally they didn't do this," he said, with a shake of his head. "But it does make me wonder who else it could have been."

"And, if it was part of this stalker group, don't you think they would have taken these photos with them?"

"That's one probability, yes," he said. "If it were me, I

would. But I guess it's possible he didn't see it, although a fair bit of destruction is in the bedroom, so it's most likely he did see it but probably didn't understand the relevance."

"But that's assuming again," she said, "that he isn't part of this or one of those names."

"But maybe he saw it as more of a trophy wall, or maybe he saw it more as something the cops would blame the dead guy for."

"That's possible too," she said. "So many possibilities but nothing that's even slightly solid."

"That's our life," he muttered.

Finally they heard the front door open, and Fallon looked up to see Quinn, slipping back inside. "Did you find her?"

"Yeah, and I did talk to her, but she wasn't too interested in talking to me about it."

"Until you turned on the great charm?" she teased.

"Well, if you say so," he said. "She did eventually open up, but it took money to make her talk."

"Right," she said. "So, when charm doesn't work, money always does."

Such a note of bitterness was in her voice that Fallon looked at her. He said, "You know that people are people, all over the world."

"I know," she said. "So, Quinn, what did she have to say?"

"They had a fight over this door of photos apparently," he said, pointing at it. "She thought they were having a relationship, until she saw the back of his door, and then she kind of lost it on him."

"Did he give her any explanation?" Fallon asked.

"Yes, he did. According to her, he said that he was just

taking photos of her for a friend."

"But she didn't believe him?" Fallon asked.

"No, not only did she not believe him but it was the reason for their breakup."

"But she came back here to apologize," Linny added.

"Yeah, she said that he was a nice guy and that she was willing to give him a second chance."

"Even though he was photographing another woman and had photos of her on the back of his bedroom door?" Linny said, frowning.

Quinn just nodded.

"Okay, that sounds pathetic," she said.

"Unless he convinced her that what he was doing was for real," Fallon said.

"Maybe." Linny frowned at that. "It's still far-fetched though."

"Which is why she broke up with him," Quinn stated. "But now she's thinking about it and can't come up with any other excuse, so she's back to giving him a second chance."

"And he didn't give her any ideas as to who wanted the photos?" Fallon asked.

"She did give me the name of who it supposedly was." He held up a small notebook, where he'd written it down.

"Interesting," she muttered, looking at Fallon. "Keith Talbot."

"Did she say where he lived?" Fallon asked Quinn.

"Apparently he's in the same building."

At that, Fallon wanted to finally shout out in joy. "Perfect. Whereabouts?"

"Two floors up," he said, as he grinned at him. "I figured you'd want to come."

"Hell yeah, I want to come. Let's go," he said, as he took

one last look around. "I don't think we need to come back here, do you?"

"I think we need to check out this Keith Talbot before anybody else gets wise to what's going on. Then we can decide if we want to come back or not to Ben's apartment."

"Right."

With that, they all three headed out, closing the door quietly behind them.

CHAPTER 6

I T WAS SUCH an odd experience to be creeping through the hallways, at night, on this secret mission. Linny was used to being up all night long anyway, particularly after having done her years in medical studies. Yet this felt so different. She was already over the fact that this young man had died, particularly after she saw the photos of herself on the back of the door. She didn't want to be crass or unfeeling, but it was hard to be sympathetic for somebody who had obviously been stalking her for years. That he died in a very strange and unknown way just added to the mystery.

As they made their way up two more floors, she said to the men, "So how will you get this guy to talk to you?"

"It's amazing what people will say when they're threatened," Quinn replied.

"Whoa, whoa, whoa," she said in alarm. "No threats here."

"Yeah, so what do you propose?" Fallon asked. "How will you get him to talk?"

She stared at him nonplussed. "I have no idea."

"Well, maybe that's something you need to think about," Quinn said. "Because we need answers, and this guy is obviously involved."

They walked down the hallway and seemed to be closer to the penthouse up here with far fewer doors. As if each apartment were much bigger.

"Interesting," she said. "The bigger places are up here. He probably has money."

"Most likely, at least some money," Fallon said. "That just adds credence to the story that the neighbor lady gave us."

As they approached the apartment in question, it opened suddenly, and a man emerged, dragging several large suitcases out in a hurry. Outside the door, seeing the two big guys, he stopped and froze. In a panic he tried to jump back inside and close the door, but his suitcases tripped him up, and he ended up on the hallway carpet.

Immediately Quinn and Fallon stationed themselves on either side and helped him to his feet. They brought the man and the luggage back inside, and, with her inside with them, they shut the door.

"Planning on going somewhere, Keith?"

He looked at them frantically, from one to the other. "I don't know who you are," he said, "but I have a plane to catch. I have to leave."

"Well, I'm sure a plane will be the first one out in the morning, but I highly doubt it's flying anywhere right now," he said.

"I have to go!" he said.

"And why is that? Maybe because your friend downstairs is dead?"

He stopped and stared, and Linny could almost see the fear ripping through him.

"I didn't have anything to do with that," he said. "I don't know anything about it."

"And what about the woman who said Ben was taking these photos for you?" Fallon asked, his voice hard.

The man's face literally turned white, ash white, as all the color slipped away. "I don't know anything about that," he cried out in a high-pitched voice.

"Meaning, you didn't hire Ben?"

Keith shook his head, then he nodded, then he shook his head, as if he were unsure of the right answer.

"Just give us the truth," Quinn said, placing a hand on the man's shoulder. "The truth, please."

"Ben was obsessed with her," he said. "Ben was obsessed with everything about her."

"And?"

Linny realized that Keith hadn't actually seen her because she stood slightly behind Fallon. Keith was so focused on the two men that he hadn't noticed her.

"Why her?"

"I don't know," he said. "I don't know. He was obsessed."

"And do you even know who she is?"

"Some broad," he said. "I mean, she was a good looker and all that."

At that, Linny stepped forward, her hands on her hips, and said, "Me, by any chance?"

He stared at her and started babbling incoherently.

She looked at Quinn. "Well, I don't usually get that kind of reaction."

With that, the guy burst into tears, sank to the floor, sobbing.

"I presume he thinks he's in trouble."

"Oh, yeah, he's in trouble all right," Linny said.

"But if he didn't kill that Ben guy—"

"I didn't kill him. I didn't kill him. I didn't kill him," he said in this endless litany. But he stared at her now, as if he

79

couldn't pull away his gaze?

Fallon immediately stepped in front of her and said, "Don't look at her." The guy quickly dropped his gaze and nodded.

"What is going on here?" she cried out. "What the hell is this?"

"You're just so beautiful," he said.

"Were you part of the stalking scenario?"

He stopped, hesitated, and then said, "I just wanted more pictures of you."

"Why?"

He looked at her in surprise. "To look at."

She stared at him for a long moment, hating the implications sliding through her mind. "Okay, so you wanted pictures, and he didn't get enough for you?"

"No, no, he was hiding a bunch, and he wanted me to pay for them."

"So he was taking pictures of me, and you wanted more, but he wanted to sell them, is that it?" She felt dirty all over again, as he nodded frantically. "So ... what? He didn't want to sell them, or you didn't want to pay?"

"Well, I was paying," he said. "I have money. I could pay. That's why he asked. I figured it was better if it was a business decision anyway."

"How do you figure that?"

"Well, because then I would have some legal standpoint, as far as ownership."

They all just stared at him.

"Okay, so they were just pictures," he cried out. "There was nothing illegal about it."

"So, why don't you take your own pictures?"

"Because I'm really bad around girls," he said. "They

won't even talk to me." His voice was so gloomy that she almost wanted to laugh.

Almost.

Fallon said, "So he was just taking pictures, and you weren't expecting Ben to kidnap her or anything like that?"

He looked at him in horror. "Oh, my gosh, no, no, no, no," he stammered. "She's beautiful, but I would never want to hurt her."

"Maybe, but lots of people have different versions of what *hurt* actually is." Even as Fallon spoke, Linny stared at him in shock.

"I hadn't even considered that," she muttered.

He nodded. "So back to you paying Ben for photos. Did you kill him when you realized he was blackmailing you for more photos?"

"I didn't kill him," he said. "I told you that." Such earnestness was in his voice, almost like he was simplistic in his belief that these men would listen and would believe his story.

She stared at him in surprise. "If you didn't kill him, did you pay him for the photos?"

"Yes," he said. "I did. Several times."

"The photos were that important?"

He nodded. "Yes," he said. "They're beautiful."

"Okay, so he was a photographer?"

"Yes, yes, yes," he said in surprise. "But isn't that why you're here, because of his photos?"

"You actually believe he's a photographer?" Quinn asked, studying the man in front of him.

"Yes, that's what he was," he said. "He had photos all over the place."

"He may have had photos," he said, "but that doesn't

mean he's a photographer."

"Well, he was really good," he said. "Really good."

"Okay, so what does *really good* mean?"

"Well, he was phenomenal," he said. "He was even getting people to do galleries for him."

At that, they stopped, shared a glance, and asked, "Did he have a warehouse or a workshop or a place of work, other than his apartment?"

The guy nodded eagerly. "Yes, yes," he said, and he gave them the address.

"Did he have a job?"

"Yes," he said and gave them the company and his boss.

"So what forums and social media did he visit?"

"Just an art forum," he said. "He was really heavily involved in that."

"By the way," she said. "How much did you pay him for the photos?"

"Oh," he said. "Thousands."

She stopped and stared at him. "I don't know if I should be flattered or insulted," she said, with a note of humor.

He looked at her in surprise. "Well, you haven't seen the nice one," he said, and he headed to his bedroom. When they didn't follow, he said, "This way, come on."

So, with Fallon leading the way, she stepped in behind him, into Keith's bedroom where a huge picture of her was blown up, the quality only somewhat bearable because it was such a large print.

"It's so unfocused," she said. "How can you even stand it?"

"It was the closest he could get."

"Yeah, you're supposed to have permission from the people in your photos," she muttered.

He looked at her in surprise. "What do you mean?"

"You can't just take photographs and blow them up of people like this," she said. "You're supposed to have permission, from the model."

"Oh," he said. "Well, maybe that's why it's so blurry. He said he was having trouble getting you to sign the paperwork." He looked at her in such distress, as he said, "Couldn't you just do that?"

"Why?"

"Because he has so many more photos of you," he said. And then he started rubbing his hands together. "If I got the forms for you, would you fill them out?"

Shocked, she took several steps back, wondering how she'd fallen into such a strange *Alice in Wonderland* tunnel. She looked at Fallon, who was studying the man in front of them.

"Why don't we go check out the rest of these addresses you've given us," he said. "Also why were you running out the door?"

"Because he's dead," he shrieked. "He's dead. He's dead. He's dead."

"And that means what?"

He stared at them in shock, looking surprised. "Well, if he's dead, what if somebody's coming after me?"

"Did you do something wrong?" Quinn asked.

"No, of course not," he said.

"So why do you think someone's coming after you?"

At that, the guy stopped, stared, and said, "Oh, do you think I'm okay then?"

"I don't know," Fallon said. "What I do know is that this guy was involved in some other stuff, and that's why he got killed."

It was like watching a cartoon, almost, as this guy understood that he wasn't in any danger.

He just smiled and let out a big sigh and said, "In that case, I'm going back to bed."

He ushered them toward the front door. "Go, go, go," he said. "It's been a very exhausting day."

"You think?" Fallon said, under his breath, but she heard him.

She turned and looked at Keith and said, "Thank you for the help."

He beamed. "You sure you won't sign those papers?"

"I think you've got enough photos of me," she said, and, with that, she stepped out into the hallway. Once outside, she turned to look at Fallon. "Was that for real?"

"Oh, it was for real all right," he said. "I can't imagine who all these other guys are that Ben's been sending photos to."

"I wonder if this Keith guy knows that other people have the same pictures."

"I don't know," Fallon said. "How are you feeling? Knowing they've got these photos and all, I mean."

"It's disturbing," she admitted. "But I'm not sure what I'm supposed to do about it."

"Well, hopefully we can get to the bottom of this," Quinn said. "And you won't have to do anything."

"I like the idea of that," she said. "That big one, blown up in the bedroom, was just—because it was so distorted and blurry, I can't imagine anybody even wanting it hung up."

"That's what's puzzling about all this," Quinn said. "I don't know what group this is that he was contacting and sending these photos to. Do you suppose the photos are all like this one?"

"I don't know," Fallon said, "but, if they are, that says something. Where does one find somebody like this Keith guy?"

"A mental hospital," she said immediately.

"Which nobody else gets access to, correct?" Fallon asked her.

She nodded. "Correct, at least in the US."

"Right," he said. "So who's to say about it over here?"

"Right, but you would hope that somebody hospitalized has confidentiality," she said, "no matter what country they are in."

"Which, as we all know," Quinn added, "is something that can also be taken care of, if people have enough money."

"Back to that whole money thing again," she muttered.

"Absolutely. So now what?" Quinn asked Fallon.

"I suggest we either head home, or we check out a couple more of these addresses."

"Well, I suggest," she said, "that we just keep going. No point in heading home for a break when we're actually finding stuff now. Every step of the way we're getting something new."

"Well, that's true enough," he said. "So let's keep going then."

"Says you," she said, with a smile.

"You don't want to go?"

"Oh, I still want to go," she said. "Pull up the address for his darkroom, and let's see how far away we are."

"Not far," he said. "Just around the corner."

"Let's go," she said. "Let's see what this sicko guy's workshop looks like."

"You won't freak out?"

"At what? More blurry photographs? No," she said.

"Definitely not. You really don't think that guy Keith is in any danger?"

"I don't think so," Fallon said. "But who knows? I've been wrong before, and this whole situation hasn't followed the typical patterns yet."

THEY GOT BACK into the vehicle and quickly drove to the new address, which literally was just around the corner. They could have walked here, but they didn't want to leave the vehicle too long in one place. As it was, just enough anger was building in his head that Fallon prided himself on having maintained the amount of calm he already had. Because, up until seeing all those photos of Linny gathered on one door, he'd thought this was something distant, basically commonplace. But seeing those photos, he realized some seriously creepy element was involved. The fact that the photos were all blurry, he wondered if that was a stylized effect that somebody had deliberately gone for, but it made somewhat better sense to him. Either way, the whole thing was just wrong.

Seeing the man Keith that they'd found on the sixth floor, and the way he'd reacted to seeing her, wanting her photographs, well, that was just creepy.

At his side, Quinn said, "Really makes you rethink things, doesn't it?"

"In many ways," he said. "I still can't figure out if those photographs were meant to be like that or—"

"I was wondering that myself. It's odd either way."

"It's all odd though," she muttered from the back seat.

"Here we are," Quinn said, as he pulled up in front of a large warehouse in a much more commercial artsy district and said, "This looks like an interesting space."

"Depends on what we find in it," Fallon said.

"Please tell me that you're not expecting dead bodies," she said.

Both men stopped and looked at her.

Quinn asked, "Why would you even bring that up?"

"Because so far we've got one," she said, "and the case has just slipped down some weird rabbit hole. I don't know how many others might be around."

"Well, let's hope not," he said, "because that's not something any of us want to deal with."

"You think?" she said, shaking her head. "I don't know where that thought came from. Just fear I guess."

At that, Fallon hooked his arm through hers and said, "You don't have to go in."

"You're not keeping me out," she said. "I mean, it's just really puzzling to see the men involved in this case. There was definitely an issue with the guy who was my admirer," she said, in that mocking tone. "He was off in some way."

"Such as?"

"It's hard to explain. I don't want to say that he was off his meds, but it kind of was that."

"Which would make perfect sense," he said. "Not that you're not plenty beautiful enough to get a lot of stalkers on your own," he said hurriedly. She just looked at him and rolled her eyes.

Quinn, on the other hand, snorted with laughter at Fallon's clumsy attempt to get his foot out of his mouth.

"Okay, enough already. I get it."

"You know," Quinn said, serious now, "somebody acting the way Keith was, it does make sense that there could be some mental instability there."

"Absolutely," she agreed. "Definitely an issue with this Keith guy."

"Or could he just be good at whatever he does and then completely creepy about a lot of other things," Quinn suggested.

"Not just guys though," Fallon corrected. "A lot of men and women are very good at what they do professionally, yet they are also socially inept. They don't have enough practice or an established skill set or some social ability to interact as you and I would," he said quietly.

"Recent conversation excluded," Quinn quipped.

"Ya think?" she said. "Seriously though, there are all kinds of proper medical terms for that kind of thing, with many nuances," she said cheerfully. "But you're right, and I'm considering that a whole lot right now."

"Well, if you come up with anything, let us know."

"Don't expect any psychiatric diagnoses from me," she said. "I'm a surgeon. I'm not somebody who studies and understands all the mind-sets of people with these kinds of mental problems."

"Did psychiatry ever interest you?"

"No," she said quickly, maybe too quickly. "It brought me a little too close to thinking about—well—the people who killed my parents."

"I guess that's one of the reasons why I was wondering if you would go into something like that," Fallon said. "Because it might help you to understand the people who did it."

"Helping me to understand the individuals, or that mind-set, didn't let me sleep at night," she said. "I learned as much as I needed to from Uncle Dave and the rest of you over the years, and I decided that my own mental health needed a completely different field."

"Good enough," he said. "We all have to make decisions for ourselves."

"Then we hopefully have enough perseverance to actually act on them and to follow through," she muttered.

He looked at her in surprise.

She shrugged. "You have no idea how many times I've wanted to quit over the years."

"I don't know of anything much harder than med school," he said. "The fact that you persevered and did make it is a huge accomplishment, and you should be very damn proud of yourself."

"I am," she said, with a nod. "Didn't make it any easier to get there though."

He chuckled at that. "No," he said. "All of us have had certain things that we've pushed ourselves for, and, when we've made it, it's been a huge blessing, but that doesn't make it any easier to get to that point, and it's not exactly something anybody else can help us with."

"No," she said, "not at all."

They stood outside the warehouse, and Fallon said, "I think I'll check around the back."

"I got it," Quinn said, already taking off in that direction. "You guys go in through the front. I'll go in through the back."

"We're expecting it to be empty, right?" she asked Fallon, as they stepped closer.

"We're expecting it to be, yes, but we can never count on something like that."

She just nodded, and he was grateful for her quiet silence and support. Once out on this road trip, she never questioned their decisions, never questioned why they were doing something; she just followed along.

"Stay behind me though," he said. "Just in case it isn't empty."

She took a deep breath at that, slowly nodded, and said, "Okay, that makes sense. Are we going in right now?"

"I'm giving Quinn a couple minutes to get into position," he said.

When his phone buzzed, he checked it—Quinn sending him a message, saying he was going in. With that, he slipped up to the front door, checked that it was locked, and quickly picked it. He pushed open the door ever-so-quietly and stepped inside, holding his hand back to keep her slightly behind him. Being protective just came naturally. Lindsey was somebody he cared about, though at this moment he wished that she were a long way away from here.

He tilted his head, as he listened to the silence around him. He felt her warm breath, she was so close to him. But his senses weren't telling him anything was wrong.

Then he sniffed and wrinkled up his nose. Maybe there was after all. But it didn't smell like what he'd expected it to, and decomp never really had anything other than that very distinctive odor. But if somebody had utilized some chemical to cover it, then that might explain this particular smell. But this was different. Definitely a chemical smell. He took a step forward cautiously, and, in the back, he heard Quinn—at least he hoped it was Quinn. Not knowing for sure, he sent out an echoey owl call.

Quinn responded quickly with his own birdcall, confirming it was him.

Fallon moved through the front part of the building, looking for a light switch. The place was dark.

"What's that smell?" Quinn said, when they met up.

"I don't know," Fallon said, his tone grim. "But we need to find out."

Just then Quinn found a light switch and turned it on, and powerful lights filled the small room, a darkroom scenario going on here.

Fallon looked at the photographs hanging on a series of strings and whistled. "Wow. They're all Linny."

"That's just beyond creepy," she muttered beside him.

He reached out with his hand, and she reached back. "Just stay calm," he said. "We'll figure it out."

"The only thing I can figure out is he took a normal-looking photograph." She pointed to one on the wall that was somewhat clear. "I'm outside one of the shops. I don't even know when he took that." She studied it for a moment and shrugged. "I think I was out shopping, with Uncle Dave."

"But that's not recent then, is it?"

"No," she said in surprise. "We haven't done that on this trip. Not since Bullard's accident," she said carefully.

Fallon nodded. "So this is somebody who knew of you from before."

"Yes, but we already knew that."

He nodded. "But it also indicates that this whole thing has most likely been going on for a while. Because he's been taking variations of that photograph and doing things to them."

She took a long slow breath. "As long as he's not thinking that what he was doing was something that he'd like to do to me."

"No, we aren't going there," he muttered.

"Good, because seeing myself in these photographs is kind of creepy."

"More than kind of," Quinn said. "It's very creepy, for all of us. Weird too."

"Right," she muttered, as they wandered through the place.

"At least the smell appears to be the various solutions he used to develop his photos."

"But I don't understand," she said. "How did he make these variations on the photograph?"

"Well, he had the negative," Fallon said. "And apparently some very old-fashioned techniques."

She nodded, as she studied them. "Each one gets a little blurrier, a little more abstract."

"I think that was the look he was going for," Quinn said. "It's not so much an art form that you would recognize nowadays, but it was an art form that had had its day, at least for these guys."

"Okay, well, that makes me feel a little better than him stalking me." But then she turned and looked at the wall of the hallway they had walked in the dark and saw several more facing her. "Or not," she said, with a heavy sigh. "Look."

They turned to see the various poses, as she got out of a vehicle, as she stood beside a vehicle, outside a shop talking with Uncle Dave, talking with various other people.

Fallon stepped closer, took a look at the photos, and asked, "These are all over here though, right?" He turned to face her. "We need to confirm that our quarry is literally located here in Africa and that he hadn't been traveling around the world after you."

She studied each of the photos and then shook her head. "No, they're all from here, but they have been taken over the last few years," she said. "At least as far as I can tell."

"That wouldn't be a big surprise," Fallon said. "It probably started fairly simply and then carried on. Without having specifics, it's hard to know just how far back his fascination went with you."

"He only contacted me a year ago, or maybe two actually," she said.

"Maybe, but that's not necessarily a short time frame," he added. "It could be a case of a stalker finding something they like, and staying quiet for a long time with that, until something triggers them. Or they can go after it with a ferocity that will surprise anybody."

"It's hard to be surprised, after everything I've seen," she said. "But this guy's surprising me."

Fallon chuckled. "I think what's fascinating is the distortions he's making to the photos. And those are the ones that he's sending around. It's almost like, 'Hey, this is me, this is what I like, this is what I'm doing. If you appreciate it, here's more.'"

"And that would be the nicest of the options," she said. "Otherwise I'm dealing with somebody who's also ridiculously crazy to have photos of me."

"Which is why we have to contact these other members and see what they're doing with the photos."

"Agreed." She turned and looked around and said, "Is there anything else we need to do here?"

Quinn came through from the other side of the room. "I'm not seeing anything of terrible interest, are you?"

"No, not particularly." Fallon looked back at her. "You ready to go home?"

"Only if we're done," she said firmly.

He gave her a long look, seeing the fatigue in her gaze and the unrest in her eyes. "It's pretty well time. We'll do one last loop back through to make sure that we're not missing out on anything," he said. And, with her at his side, he did a quick sweep, checking drawers, checking the tabletop.

"You think the cops will come in here?"

"They should," he said. "If not, we'll direct them."

"Good, it'd be nice if all this were destroyed," she muttered.

"We'll see what we can do about that too."

"I was thinking," Quinn said, "that we should set up a camera, see if anybody comes here after all these treasures."

"That would imply that somebody knew where this Ben guy developed his photos," she said, frowning.

"Keith did. Why wouldn't somebody else come here to see his creations?" he said. "Think about it."

"Right, somebody obviously knows what Ben's been doing, so they could potentially have followed him to get more information."

Quinn nodded. "But we don't have the video equipment with us."

"But we can get it easily enough," Fallon said. "Let's head back home. If we decide to do this, I'll grab what I need, and I'll come back here and set it up."

"Or I'll come. In the meantime, let's make sure we set the door, so we can tell if anybody has come in," Quinn muttered.

CHAPTER 7

LINNY WATCHED AS they set up the door, so they knew if somebody had come through or not. She thought it was a string they'd used but then realized it was a hair, so small and so insignificant that most people wouldn't have a clue that it was even there. "That's a tricky way to do it, isn't it?"

"It's fairly commonplace, so some people might be looking for it, but only if they're doing the kind of work we are."

"Which most of them probably aren't," she said, with a nod of her head.

"Not likely, no."

"But that doesn't mean it's a given."

"Right."

She smiled as they walked back to the vehicle. "I don't even know how to feel," she said, "except relieved."

"That he's dead or that you found the source of the photos?"

"Both maybe. I know that doesn't make me a very good person, but, if Ben's dead, he won't cause me any more trouble."

"Exactly, which is why a lot of people think murder is the best solution to their problems."

"Gruesome, but yeah," she said.

"Come on. Let's go home."

She turned and followed Fallon back to the SUV. The

drive was quiet, Fallon in the driver's seat, and Quinn typing away on his phone. "Well, Ben's employer is out of business. Shut down over nine months ago. So one less place to check out."

When they parked in the garage at the compound, she looked at the men and said, "I'll go to bed."

"Who's going back with the camera?" Fallon asked Quinn.

Quinn nodded. "I'll head back."

Fallon motioned at Lindsey. "I'll stand watch."

"Why do you have to stand watch?" she said. "Why does anybody have to stand watch?"

"Because it's what we do," Fallon said. "I'll help him collect the stuff he needs to get this job done."

"Shouldn't you go with him then?"

"No," he said firmly. "Go on. Get to bed."

She glared at him but realized there wouldn't be any point in talking to him. Considering that the darkroom was basically empty, she wasn't sure Quinn would be in any danger either. "You really should call somebody else back here, so you have an extra person," she said.

"That would be nice, but it's not necessarily an option right now."

"I thought there were some guys in Australia."

"They're involved in locating Bullard," he said. "That's a priority. We don't want anybody pulled off that."

"I thought they were also helping you."

"They are," Fallon said, with a smile.

"Says you." She rolled her eyes at him.

"It is what it is," he said. "So don't worry about it."

She headed up to bed, her mind still consumed with the photos that she'd seen. Such an odd thing. When she got up to her room, she checked her laptop for emails and messages, trying to find a way to unwind. But one stopped her in her tracks. She immediately got up, dressed, then with her laptop in her hand, she headed down to where Fallon worked in front of the command center console.

He turned to look at her in surprise. "What's up?"

Wordlessly, she held out her laptop. "I was just checking on my emails to see if I needed to be dealing with anything," she said, "when I saw this one."

He looked at it in surprise, quickly scrolled down, and said, "Interesting."

"That's all you've got to say?" she asked in surprise.

"Well, there is no such thing as a big surprise over something like this," he said. "The fact is, this creepy dude has got a copy of one of the photos."

"I've never had any email from him before."

"I don't think it's the same photo," he said.

She frowned at that.

"It looks like one of the photos that we saw hanging in the darkroom," Fallon noted.

"So, did this get sent before our dead guy ended up dead, or did this get sent afterward?" she asked. "In that case, it could be from the killer."

He looked at her in surprise, immediately pulled out his phone, and contacted Quinn. When his buddy picked up the phone, Fallon said, "Go in easy. We've got an email here on Lindsey's laptop with one of the photographs we saw hanging there earlier."

"Meaning?"

"Meaning someone's likely had access to that space."

"You mean, since the dead guy showed up?"

"Yes."

"Shit," he said. "Put Linny on?"

"I'm here," she said, realizing he didn't know the phone was on Speaker. "I checked my emails and saw it just now."

"Good enough," he said. "I'll check first to make sure that nobody has been inside since we were gone, and then I'll set up a camera. This is actually good news."

"It's only good news," she said in exasperation, "if you take care of yourself and don't get caught by this guy."

"Wasn't planning on it," he said cheerfully. "I'll check in. Give me a few minutes though."

And, with that, the line went silent.

She looked at Fallon. "I'm not sleeping now."

He frowned at her. "You need some sleep," he said gently.

"Now my mind's all hyped up again."

"That's why we never check emails," he said, with a laugh. "But, if you're not going to sleep, do you want to put on some coffee?"

"That I can do." She headed into the kitchen and quickly put on a pot for them. When she walked back in, she asked, "Has Quinn checked in yet?"

Fallon shook his head.

She frowned. "Shouldn't he be there now?"

"I would have thought so, yes."

She watched as he sent a text message to Quinn. They waited and waited but nothing. "How long do we wait?" she asked hoarsely.

"What would you like to do," he asked, "if he doesn't answer?"

"We're going there after him," she said. "You know we are."

He brushed the hair off his face.

"We're not leaving him," she said.

"That's certainly not something I would do normally," he said. "But I also don't want to take you into danger." He started clicking on the console.

"You already said nobody was close enough to help out."

"No, I don't think anybody is," he said. "But that doesn't mean I'm necessarily correct. Maybe somebody is around here who can look after you."

"I'm not somebody who needs to be looked after," she snapped.

"I get it," he said, "but I'm not taking you into a dangerous situation."

She took a long slow deep breath. "You don't have any choice," she said. "Quinn hasn't answered, and that means he's in trouble."

FALLON GRAPPLED WITH the problem at hand. But, as his worry for Quinn grew, he said, "Come on. Let's go," and he bolted for the door.

"Are you sure it's safe?" she asked.

"What? That we're going after him or that you're coming with me? Isn't it a little late to worry?" He quickly loaded up the weapons that he had left in the front closet, snatched them up, and headed to the garage. "Come on. Come on."

But she was already there at his side. "You're really worried, aren't you?"

"I don't like anything about this now," he said. "It's that email. That changes everything. I should never have sent him back out again."

"You didn't," she said quietly. "You guys are used to operating and working alone, so this is nothing different."

"No, this is different," he snapped. "It's still ... I don't like having to worry about you at the same time."

"Well, it is what it is."

Inside the vehicle, they took off, the engine as powerful as ever, as it churned beneath her feet. As they headed out on the road, she asked, "Do you have anybody you can call on?"

"Outside of calling the cops, not really," he said.

"Then I'll call Wagner again. Uncle Dave counted on Wagner."

"Only when there was nobody else," he said.

"Good enough," she said.

"You might want to keep the hour in mind."

"I don't give a damn if I get him out of bed or not," she said. And, sure enough, a sleepy voice answered. She quickly explained the situation, and his voice came alive almost instantly. "I presume you guys are on your way there now?"

"We are, but we're not sure what we might come up against when we get there," she said.

"You could have told me about finding his little photography room earlier," he snapped.

"Well, we would have, but it was only an hour or two ago, and we were waiting for morning. But next time we'll be sure to wake you up over things like that too."

He groaned. "Don't start with me," he said.

"Are you coming?"

"I'm jumping into my shoes now," he said. "I'll be there in ten." And he hung up on her.

She looked at Fallon and said, "Well, it's somebody anyway."

"I know," he said.

They pulled up to the warehouse they'd been at earlier.

"Did you see the car?"

He nodded. "Yeah, it's right there."

"Good, that's something."

"Doesn't make a whole lot of difference at this point," he said.

"Maybe it does. Let's check."

"We're not going there," he said. "He's not in the vehicle. I drove past it already."

"Fine." She waited, while he got out, and then she stepped around behind him. They checked the front door.

He said, "The hair is still there."

"So where did Quinn go?"

"Probably around the back." He frowned at the thought, then looked at her.

"No, I'm going with you. But let's go in through the back, since that's where we're likely to find him."

They quickly made their way around to the back of the building, and there they found the rear door open. Fallon pulled out a weapon, and, keeping her behind him, he stepped slowly inside. He heard slight sounds going on inside but nothing very obvious. He wasn't sure if it was a mouse rustling in the dark corners, if it was Quinn and his phone was dead, or if it was somebody else.

Then they heard a voice. "Thought you would come in and steal my photos, did you?"

And Fallon realized somebody actually had Quinn. Fallon waited and listened. But he heard nothing else, except some strange noises, as if this stranger was, he hated to say it, was almost growling. With her quietly staying close behind, he moved in to where they could see more. Once there, he saw Quinn, completely flat on the floor and seemingly unconscious. That didn't mean he was though. It was the standard procedure that, if you were taken captive, you should appear totally knocked out, while you made escape or attack plans. Another guy was there, quite small, busily collecting the photos.

"These are mine. Paid for by me. You're not stealing them."

Fallon stepped forward, his handgun in front of him, and said, "Yet you're stealing them now."

The man turned and gasped. He immediately jerked his hands in the air, and the photos plummeted to the floor. But the stranger wasn't looking at Fallon. Our stranger was staring at Lindsey, beside Fallon. A look of complete rapture on his face.

"It's you. Oh, my God. It's you." And he raced forward.

She stepped behind Fallon, who raised the weapon, and said, "Stop."

The guy looked at him, his lower lip quivering, then stared at the weapon. "Are you hurting her?" he said.

"No," Fallon said, "of course not. But you've damn well hurt my friend." Linny was already over there, gently checking out Quinn's head wound, not wanting to wake him up yet.

"Your friend?" he said. "That's not fair. He came in here, trying to steal my photos."

"But they're not your photos either," he said. "Are they?"

At that, the man looked stunned and said, "Yes, they are."

"No, they aren't," she said. "They belong to Ben Radcliffe, don't they?"

He stared. "I paid for them," he said. "These were supposed to be mine."

"You mean that one or two of them were supposed to be yours. But he was selling them to a lot of people. Actually he was giving a lot away too. Did that bother you?"

"Of course it bothered me. I was paying for mine."

"And so were others. Interesting that you prefer the really distorted versions."

"No, no, no. He was … He was somebody who was well ahead of his time," he said, and every word that came out of his face was seriously normal sounding. But the look on his face as he stared at the photos revealed that he was more than a little addicted to whatever drug he was on.

"So what's your name?" Fallon asked.

"Peter."

Fallon wondered at the ease of getting info from this guy. Wondered if it was because of the drugs he was on; then he wondered if it was something else because there was just no understanding his behavior. "I'll walk over and check on my friend," he said. "I want you to walk back over there and stand where your photos are."

"Yes, yes," he said. "My photos." He raced back over and quickly collected the ones that had dropped on the floor.

Fallon bent down and nudged Quinn with his foot. Quinn moaned slightly. "Quinn, wake up," he said. "We've got company."

Immediately Quinn's eyes flew open, and he stared around in surprise, then slowly made his way to his knees as he studied the new player in the game. He looked at the stranger and said, "You the one who hit me?"

"No, no, no," he said, "I didn't hit you. I was protecting my photos."

"Right, protecting them by hitting me," he said in a dry tone.

The guy nervously went back to collecting them and held them clutched against his chest. "You might have taken them," he said.

"Well, that's not likely, when I came here to preserve them," he said.

At that, the other man said, "Are you one of her fans too?"

"Sure, I am apparently," he said. "How did you find out about it?"

"The website," he said. "It's such a beautiful website with all those photos."

At that, Fallon turned to look at Linny. "Website?"

She shook her head ever-so-slowly. "I haven't got a clue what he's talking about."

"Yes, yes, yes," he said. "The one where you do all the modeling."

"No," she said.

"What's the website address?" Fallon asked.

"Well, it's one of the hidden ones," he said. "We can only get to it from the forum."

"Great, what forum is that?" he asked, and the man supplied the name of it easily enough.

"You realize that's like an art forum," she said.

Peter looked at her and said, "Well, of course, this is all art. You didn't think it was something else, did you?" He looked at her, completely affronted. "What do you mean? What are you talking about?"

She shook her head, brought up her phone, and checked for the website. When it loaded, it said something about not being a real website. "What's the forum again?"

He gave her the URL for that.

"I'm not a member, so it won't let me in. Give me your log-in, so I can check out my website."

He quickly gave it to her, without argument. Fallon was

surprised because either this guy was seriously innocent or had no clue what was involved here. She brought it up and, sure enough, saw the same photos that they'd seen in the house on the back of Ben's bedroom door and now in his darkroom.

"You mean, all these photos?" Fallon said, pointing to them.

Peter stepped up and nodded. "Yes, these are the originals. They're all of her." He smiled. "We're so happy to have you on board."

"Wrong," she said. "Those pictures were taken of me when I wasn't aware of it."

"Yes, that makes it much better," he said. "Of course it'd be easier if you would sign the forms." He looked at her and fretted. "Haven't you signed them?"

"I haven't even seen them," she said. "So have you done this before? Had photos of a different woman up there, and he does these variations of art on the photos?"

"Yes," he said. "We have several women whose photos we'd really like to have."

He gave such a happy sigh that they all just stared at him in shock.

By now Quinn had regained his feet and was leaning against one of the walls. No blood poured down his head, but he looked a little sore and pissed. Mostly pissed. He stared at the guy in front of him. "You realize that the photographer is dead, right?"

"Yes, I heard," he said. "That's why I'm here, getting my pictures."

"Yet I don't think they're your pictures."

"No, I told you that I paid for them."

"And you can prove that?"

"Yes, of course," he said. "All the transactions went through my bank."

"Good," said a new voice to this conversation. "Then you won't mind explaining it to us."

And, sure enough, Wagner walked in.

He took one look at the gathered crowd and said, "So I needn't have come after all?"

"This guy attacked Quinn here," said Fallon. "Knocked him out cold, and he's been collecting all these photos, saying they are his. Basically they're all pictures of Linny here."

"What?" Wagner stepped forward, frowning. "Seriously?" He looked at the walls, as Fallon pointed them out, and then at all the distorted art versions of the photographs. "Wow," he said, looking at the stranger. "And you were just protecting the photographs, I presume, when you attacked Quinn here?"

"Of course," he said. "This is art."

"Right," he said. Wagner looked back at Quinn. "You okay?"

"Yeah," Quinn growled. "But this place is getting too *looney tuney* for me. I'll go outside and grab some fresh air."

"Maybe I'll come with you," Linny said, "if you don't mind."

He reached out an arm, and she slung hers through it and followed him out. Fallon watched the two of them go quietly. He'd never seen anything but camaraderie between them, but now he found himself watching her a little more closely.

"So what do you want to do?" Wagner asked Fallon, while staring at the intruder.

"We need to confirm his story for one. Apparently

they're using a members-only website, and the photographer had been posting photos of Linny and then making these art variations. These guys are all paying for them in some way, … though it appears Ben was also just giving away some of the photos."

"He would sell the first abstraction of the photos," Peter said. "They were the better of them. Then, as the quality deteriorated, he would just give away those later versions," the guy said.

"Okay, and how do you know that the quality has deteriorated?" Fallon asked.

"Well, of course they have. Every time you take new variations of the photograph, it gets worse."

Fallon nodded. "Sure. You know they're digital, right?"

The guy looked at him in surprise. "Of course you wouldn't understand," he said, with a shake of his head. "I can see the disbelief on your face right now. Figures. It takes real, … *real* talent to appreciate art like this."

"Right," Wagner said. "Well, we'll take you down to the station, and we'll have a little talk and see what else you might have been involved in."

"I'm not involved in anything," he said. "Why would you even think that?"

"Because the authorities are looking to see who killed the photographer, Ben," Fallon said quietly.

"Well, I certainly didn't," he said. "Why would I kill off the source of all my photos?"

At that, Fallon was stumped because Peter was right. Anybody who was addicted to these pictures wouldn't have wanted to kill off the creator. No matter how Fallon tried, that logic was irrefutable. He turned toward Wagner and said, "All yours."

CHAPTER 8

OUTSIDE LINNY TOOK several slow deep breaths, as she rotated her shoulders and her neck, trying to ease up the tension clawing at the base of her throat and at the top of her shoulders.

"You okay?" Quinn asked.

She smiled. "Shouldn't I be asking you that?"

"I don't know. The guy came right behind me. Kind of disconcerting," he said. "I wasn't ... Even though I was half expecting to see something, nobody had come in through the front, so I didn't expect anybody to be coming up behind me. I was sloppy."

"You're tired," she corrected. "That's understandable."

"Doesn't matter," he said. "It's not acceptable in this world. This kind of mistake gets you killed."

"Well, they didn't kill you this time, thankfully," she said.

"Maybe not, but, at the same time, I'm not terribly impressed with myself."

"And you've got the headache to prove it." She smiled knowingly.

"Isn't that the truth."

"Still, at least he's here, and we've got him talking," she said.

"Now if only we could understand what the hell he is

even saying," Quinn said, with a grin.

At that, they both shared a laugh.

"Pretty bizarre, if you ask me."

"I guess it's just another art form," she said. "But it's kind of odd to think that they're making art by distorting the photos."

"But that's what art really is, I guess. Taking something and putting your own twist on it," he said. "They've done it since time began."

"Abstract art in painting is something we've accepted for a long time. So why not abstract photography?"

"Exactly, and apparently this guy had his own little following," Quinn said.

"So was it one of the fan club who killed Ben? And, if so, why drop him off at the compound?"

"That's the million-dollar question," he said. "And how does any of this relate back to us. We get that it relates to you, but is there a completely simple, yet obvious, answer for whoever did this? That Ben should be dropped off in front of your place, since he'd already spent his life here?"

"Well, that's kind of creepy," she muttered.

"Yep, it is. The whole thing is creepy. I didn't explain it very well, but, if Ben is the type to die for his art, that's the kind of thing he would do, isn't it?"

"And that's even worse," she said.

Quinn chuckled. "We've all seen an awful lot in life that doesn't make any sense. This could be just another one of those."

"Maybe," she muttered. "But still, you'd like to think you could latch on to something logical there."

"But isn't that what you found out before? That there's just nothing sane to latch on to?"

110

"I guess. It's still distressing."

"Yep. I get it," he said. "Just not that easy to figure out."

"No," she said. "It isn't. Still, it is what it is."

Quinn chuckled. "I'm ready to go home and to get some sleep. How about you?"

"Yeah, me too," she said, "but we'll have to tear Fallon away from inside."

Just then Fallon stepped out and looked at the two of them. "Wagner will take Peter down to the station for the night. They'll grill him and see what kind of connections he might have had, see whether it's possible that he's the one who dropped off Ben's body at the compound."

"Oh, speaking of which," Quinn said, "it doesn't look like Ben died here either."

"Nor in his apartment," Fallon said. "Not enough blood."

"So, we still don't have a crime scene yet," Quinn noted.

"No, unless it's the drop-off vehicle because a fair bit of blood was found there."

"And who drove the vehicle is another question."

"I highly suspect we'll find that it's one of the people in this artsy crowd."

"So completely unrelated to Bullard then?" Quinn asked Fallon.

"I don't know," Fallon said. "Until we get to the bottom of it, the answer will have to be a maybe."

She snorted at that. "With that ounce of wisdom," she said, "why don't we head home and get some sleep."

"It's almost morning," he said. "Maybe we should just skip the night's rest."

"Maybe you can, but I can't do that," she said. "I'm really good at power napping, and running for a few hours on a thirty-minute nap, even a ten- or fifteen-minute nap, but I can't skip it completely."

"And it's not necessary," Quinn said. "Let's go home."

As they drove back, she sank against the seat and said, "I wonder if it's all because of Uncle Dave. He's the one who warned Ben off. Maybe the photographer told the rest of the group that he'd been warned off."

"Oh," Fallon said, "now that's a possibility."

"It makes as much sense as anything," Quinn said. "How verbal was Dave?"

"Very," she said. "He caught Ben on the compound property, really irate that somebody had been bothering me, had followed me home. Uncle Dave ordered me into the compound, while he chewed him out."

"Of course," Fallon said. "You only have to think about the role he's played in your life to understand that."

"Maybe, and I wasn't there to hear the exchange, so I don't know how bad it was. But I could see their body language during that conversation. The question is whether anybody was there with them at the time."

"Interesting. So that's definitely something we can ask Dave about," he said, as he checked his watch. "Potentially as soon as we get home. That would be our first place to look."

"Exactly," she said. Just then they pulled into the compound, with gates and doors opening, then locking behind them as they headed to the garage.

As they walked inside, she watched as Fallon checked the front door. "Did you do the same thing here?"

"Absolutely," he said. "Also, before I go to sleep, I'll also check the security cameras, to ensure we didn't have any visitors while we were gone."

"Right," she said. "You do you—I'm heading off to

bed." With that, she was more than delighted to turn her back on the whole mess and headed upstairs to her room.

"LET'S RUN THROUGH that videotape," Fallon said, "and see what we're looking at."

Together, the two men searched the security cameras for the time frame from dinner forward. But found nothing.

"On that note, let's make sure we're locked down and get some sleep."

Quinn agreed.

"I also need to call Dave."

"You do that," Quinn said. "Me, I'm crashing. My head's killing me."

"You sure you don't want to get that checked, just in case?"

"Very sure," he said. "That's the last thing I want to deal with."

"Maybe," he said. "But, if it's a major injury, we can't take that chance."

"No way," he said. "You know how I feel about doctors."

"You feel the same way we all do," Fallon said, with a laugh. "But that won't necessarily help. I'd just feel a lot better to know that your head is okay."

"Well, you won't get that reassurance from me until tomorrow morning. Linny might look at it. In the meantime, I just have a lousy headache."

Fallon watched worriedly as Quinn headed up the stairs. As soon as he was out of sight and hearing, Fallon quickly phoned Dave.

Dave answered, his voice exhausted. "Is everything

okay?" he asked. "Why are you calling at this hour?" Fallon quickly filled in Dave on the evening's events. "Wow," he said. "That's terrible."

"What I want to know from you," he said, "is if you have any idea who might have done this."

"It's hard to even remember," he said. "I talked to that guy a couple times, on the phone, but the last time, in person? Well, I came pretty close to beating the crap out of him. He'd driven in and was trying to get a picture of her."

"You didn't mention that before," Fallon said, pinching the bridge of his nose. "We found all kinds of photos in his little darkroom."

"But were they recent photos?"

"Yes, taken off the street, pictures of her getting in another vehicle, things like that."

"Well, good," he said, with relief. "I don't think I could stand it if I thought some asshole had been accessing the house."

"We found two bugs inside the compound, but no evidence of any photos taken from inside," Fallon said. "Was anyone else with Ben, when you spoke to him?"

"Another guy but I don't know who he was. I honestly didn't pay much attention. I was much more concerned about the fact that I finally had Ben there in my hand."

Fallon could completely understand that. Nothing like the satisfaction of knowing your quarry was right there, ready for you to pound into the ground, if need be. He understood Dave's complete panic at seeing his niece in a compromising position or being bothered by somebody troublesome.

"Well, I understand all that," Fallon said. "But, if I had any idea of who was with Ben," he said, "he would be high on my list, and the next one I'd want to check out."

"You know what?" Dave said. "He was a small guy."

"How small?"

"At first, I thought it was just a kid, but I think he was probably thirty or so. I don't know. I remember thinking that he still had acne, like a teenager. And I was kind of pissed off, thinking that somebody else was going after her."

"But did he give any inclination of giving a damn?"

"Honestly the guy was kind of creepy. Something wasn't normal about him."

"Well, that jives with what we found so far," he said. "I'll keep digging. You keep looking for Bullard."

"Oh, don't worry. That's all I'm doing. The first two men were a no. I have to travel to a different set of islands to see about the third."

"Good searching," he said. With that, the two men rang off. Fallon made his way up to bed and, just as he walked past her room, Linny opened her door. He looked at her in surprise. "Can't sleep?"

"You were talking to Uncle Dave. Did he have anything to offer?"

"Only something about the other guy who had been with Ben, when Dave confronted them. Dave said he was small and thought at the time he had teenage acne, but, in hindsight, realized the guy was probably thirtysomething."

"So could be another one of the group members then," she said.

"That's tomorrow's work," he said, "and technically I've got the team on it already."

"Good," she said, with a bright smile. "Maybe I can sleep now."

"I was hoping you already were asleep."

"Not yet," she said. Then she turned and headed back inside her room.

He was left with an image of her long sleek back and creamy skin. He shook his head, as he walked into his room. "Great, glad she can sleep because now I need a shower." But he laughed at himself because it was no different than it ever had been. She'd always been deadly to his senses, and only due to his self-control and his respect for Dave, had Fallon held back.

Quinn had called Linny *Fallon's fatal flaw*, saying, if it were any other woman, Fallon would have made a move a long time ago. But he didn't want to upset Dave or the status quo. Quinn was right, and Fallon still wasn't sure what he was supposed to do about it. But he figured it would be something he'd have to deal with, sooner or later, given the attraction between them. At least on his part.

But, as he thought about the look in her eye, as she'd studied him, he realized it was definitely a two-way street. And somehow that just made it all that much harder to go to his lonely bed all alone. But determined to still be as honorable as possible in a situation where everything could still go to hell in a handbasket, he knew he needed sleep more than trying to clear the air and seeing just where the cards fell. He could do that later. Provided he kept her safe enough that there would be a later.

CHAPTER 9

L INNY WOKE UP bright and early and twisted in the bed slightly for a better position, groaning as her body ached from the lack of a good sleep.

"Not that I wouldn't give up sleep for some better activities to enjoy," she muttered. Of course what she should have done last night was made a move on Fallon, but he'd looked so tired and worn out that she didn't want to start something that might not go in the direction they both wanted it to go. Obviously they had some issues to sort out between them, but, as she had known from her conversation with Uncle Dave, Fallon cared, and cared a lot. That's why he stayed away.

She didn't understand that and struggled to work her way through Uncle Dave's explanation, but, when she finally did get it, her uncle had suggested she would never change it, due to the abundance of honor Fallon possessed. She understood that, and it was a hard point to argue, but, at the same time, she was also fed up with it. She'd told Uncle Dave flat-out, "Fallon's got this week. Before I leave to go home, I'll shake up his resolve a whole lot more than I've ever done before. I need to know if anything's there or not."

Now that it was morning, and she was somewhat rested, she wondered about walking into his room and crawling into his bed. Chances were, he was already up and having coffee though. And, of course, Quinn was still in the house. That wouldn't bother her though because he already understood the lay of the land. She was well past being embarrassed about it. What she didn't want to do was have any more time go by without one of them making a move. She herself had had a million excuses as to why she shouldn't have a relationship with Fallon, but, now that she was here, she didn't want to lose what could be a potentially life-changing event—something that she'd wanted for a very long time.

She'd always struggled with short-term relationships but had had a few, if for only stress relief during the years of rigorous schooling she had just completed. Still, a certain level of exhaustion remained in her system that she was worried about, but she was getting there. She just needed a little bit longer to relax and to rest up. If this nightmare around her would give her a break, that would be awesome, but the chances of it happening weren't looking all that great right now.

That was too damn bad because it was getting seriously ridiculous. She needed to go home soon, but she did have a little bit more time, though she hadn't let anybody know that. Her uncle knew, but she didn't know if he'd passed it on to the others.

She threw back the covers and groaned as she slid out of bed and headed for a hot shower. As soon as she was clean and wrapped up in a towel, she headed back to her room, studying the few items of clothing she had brought with her. She always traveled light, but she hadn't done laundry yet, so her clean clothing options were looking a little meager. But she would make it work.

When she was dressed and ready, she made her way down to the kitchen, hearing only silence around her. When she got there, she frowned and touched the coffeemaker, finding it warm, so a pot had already come and gone. So the men were up, even though she hadn't necessarily heard them. Feeling a little disgruntled to be the last one moving, early as it was, she put on another pot of coffee and opened up the fridge, looking for something to eat, for a whole lot more sustenance than she'd had of late.

She pulled out eggs and bacon. As soon as she had bacon frying, the two men drifted toward her. Sniffing the air, Quinn said, "That smells good."

"Nothing like the smell of bacon," Fallon added.

"I know, right?" she said. As she turned and gave them both a bright smile, she studied Fallon's face. "How are you two doing?"

"We're good," Quinn said. "And, yes, I'm fine."

She smiled. "How many times have you had to answer to Fallon over your head injury?"

Quinn rolled his eyes and laughed.

She smiled. "At least you know he cares."

"He's a nag," Quinn said. "But you're right." He sat down at the counter and asked, "How long until food?"

"I gather you're hungry?"

"Yep, we would cook, but we didn't want to wake you," he said.

"You could have, if you were hungry," she said.

"We weren't that hungry, and, besides, you do bacon better than I do," Quinn said.

"It's hard not to do bacon right," she said. "It's pretty damn easy actually."

"It is," they both said cheerfully.

"But we were working anyway," Quinn said.

"Any progress?"

"Not sure," Fallon said. "We're tracking the art forum and all its members. A bunch came and went over the last few years."

"Yeah, well, that makes sense," she said. "Especially if some are disinterested or if some are special needs patients, like Keith."

"They all seem to be photography buffs. A lot of them have uploaded their own photos, and they look very, ... well, not all that different from these."

She looked at him in surprise.

"I know," Fallon said. "I'm kind of surprised too, but apparently it's an art form, at least for this group."

"Good," she said. "Then it's not sexualized?"

"No, it doesn't appear to be."

"Except for? Come on. What's that I hear in your voice?"

"Well, the problem is," he said, "we can't necessarily prove that they don't have an interest that goes deeper."

"Of course not," she said. As soon as the bacon was looking almost done, she started the eggs.

"I'll have three," Quinn said.

"Are you that hungry?"

"Yeah," he said, "I'm starving."

"Okay," Fallon said, "I'll have three too."

By the time she had all the eggs on the plates, and they sat down to eat, she asked, "Is there anything I can do to help with the research?"

"I think we got it," Fallon said. "But, if there is, I'll let you know."

"Do that," she said. "I don't remember ever seeing any guy with pimples or acne, like my uncle was talking about though."

"He said the guy was in the vehicle, so he wasn't sure how involved he was in all of this anyway."

"Maybe not at all. Maybe he was just a friend, along for the ride."

"Well, that's what we're looking into," he said. "We're also trying to get the camera feeds from that warehouse area, to see who's coming and going in and out of that darkroom where Ben developed his photos."

"That's a good idea," she said, with a nod. "What about Ice? Can they help at all?"

"We sent what we had so far to them this morning," Quinn said. "They'll give us what help they can, though they're all kinds of shorthanded at the moment."

"Right," she said, with a smile. "A new baby, who would have thought?"

"Not me," Quinn said, "though it seems so strange to not have expected it. While now married, Ice and Levi have been together for a very long time."

"I like that," she said, with a smile. "It redeems my belief in humanity in a way, you know?"

"It's the cycle of life, isn't it?" Quinn said. She nodded and dug into her eggs a little more. When they were finally done, Quinn excused himself and said, "I'll head off and see what that search came up with."

"I'll join you in a minute," Fallon said, "as soon as I'm done eating."

"No rush," he said.

Quinn left them alone, and Fallon looked at her and asked, "Did you get any sleep?"

"Eventually," she admitted. "But it was kind of hard. How 'bout you?"

"Like you, eventually I got some sleep," he said, with a

smile. "But it wasn't that easy originally. I had a hot shower, and that helped."

"Me too," she said, with a smile. "I just felt kind of dirty after being in that warehouse."

"Understood." He finished his plate, pushed it back. She got up and refilled their coffee. They didn't often get a chance for just the two of them to sit together. "When are you leaving?" he asked.

"Well, I thought about leaving immediately," she said. "Now I'm thinking I want to stick around until this is done."

"*If* it's done," he said. "I can't guarantee a quick resolution."

"Well, you'll have to," she said. "I can stay a while longer—and had planned to originally—but I still have to go home eventually."

"Is New York home?"

"It is, until I'm done with my education," she said. "These internships are hard to get. At least the ones I wanted," she said. "So I want to make sure I get the best value I can."

"Understood," he said, smiling. "Who would have thought you'd end up being a doctor?"

"Me," she said, with a bright laugh. "Being here has been great, and, in many ways, I owe everybody here so much. But it was also a dream, once I realized what Bullard was doing for all the people here."

"Got it," he said. "Lots of hospitals around here could use your services."

"Maybe that's where I'll end up," she said lightly. "I just don't know yet."

"Good point." At that, he seemed to settle back slightly.

She watched as he then got up and carried his plate to the sink. "So what are we doing about us?" she asked, watching him carefully.

He froze, rinsed his dishes, and put them into the dishwasher. He then turned and looked at her and said, "There is no us."

She smiled at that. "You know what? I never took you for a liar."

He just glared at her.

"Come on. Anybody can see what's between us," she said. "I get it. When I was here before and I was younger, it was all about making sure you didn't cross those lines, or whatever it was that mattered to you. But now we're both adults, and Uncle Dave already knows how I feel. And I think everybody knows how you feel."

He's stiffened at that but didn't say a word.

"Again, back to that denial. And again, I get it. And I was prepared, I thought, to just leave once more, without bringing it up, but I've changed my mind."

"What changed your mind?"

"You," she said cheerfully. "I decided I didn't want to spend another year wondering if something between us was worth pursuing."

He sat down with a hard *thump* and stared at her.

She reached across, grabbed his hand, and said, "At least be honest with me."

"Honesty leads to trouble," he said, his voice thick.

"It can also lead to good things," she said. "In our case, we would need honesty because of the way we've both spent our lifetimes. It's the only thing that would work for us."

"But you're leaving," he said.

She laughed at that. "And you'll be leaving too. On

again, off again, at least," she said. "So that's really no different."

He frowned at that.

"I know. You're trying to get all the details out of the way, as an argument," she said. "But I'm not listening to the arguments."

"Why not?" he asked in confusion.

At that, she burst out laughing. "Because," she said, "obviously I see things a little more clearly than you do."

"In what way?" he asked, wary. Backing away from the conversation, as so many men did.

"Because we both care," she said. "We've both avoided a relationship, trying not to upset the status quo, but the status quo no longer applies."

"It applies even more right now," he said, "because of all the chaos that's going on."

"There is no chaos, Fallon," she said. "Call it what it is—loneliness, loss, and a horrible sense of grief."

He frowned at that.

"I'm not trying to fill that void," she said, "and I'm not trying to preempt anything, no matter what comes of the search for Bullard. What I'm trying to tell you is that I've waited long enough. And it's up to you if you want to take that next step or not. Me, well, you now know how I feel. So what I want from you is honesty as to how you feel."

He opened his mouth and closed it again.

"I get that it's all about honor. It's all about respect and looking after me, as part of the family. But sometimes things happen beyond our control, and this connection we have is one of those things. We've both stomped a lid down on our feelings for a very long time. I'm not prepared to do that any longer, so just tell me how you feel."

"And what if it changes everything?"

She looked at him in surprise. "It will change everything," she said. "If it's a no, then I probably won't come back here for a while. It will give me time to adjust and to become completely blasé about seeing you again. In the meantime, I'll be fine. But, if it's a yes, of course it will change everything—and for the better. Because everybody around us will feel much happier that we finally got it together."

At that, she laughed. "So, what do you have to say?"

FALLON STARED AT her, shocked. But inside was a certain amount of relief. She watched his expression, and he saw the knowing settling in. "Yes, there's something between us," he said cautiously. "But that doesn't mean it's something we should move forward on."

She chuckled. "Any reason why not? And how long were you planning on waiting?"

He stared off in the distance and then shrugged. "I didn't give it a time limit," he said. "I just put it off the table as not being a good idea, and I tend to listen to my own advice."

"You've always been a very black-and-white kind of guy," she said. "Isn't it time to shift that a little?"

"It's held me in good stead," he said. "So why would I?"

"Because you're alone, you're lonely."

"I didn't say that," he rejected immediately.

But he knew that, no matter what he said, she wasn't listening. She had her own idea of how this was supposed to play out. "Besides, what do you see us doing?" he asked. "Do you really think your uncle will be happy?"

"He already knows how I feel," she said, with a smile. "So, yes, I think he would be happy. Happy that we finally made a decision to test the water."

"And if it doesn't work out? How would that be a good thing for anybody?"

"Do you only go forward if you have a guarantee of success?"

He frowned, uncomfortable with that question. "I generally only go in the direction that looks successful."

"Years ago, that might have been the direction you followed," she said gently. "But it hardly applies today."

He wasn't quite ready to give up his position though.

She sighed. "I get it. You're scared."

"I'm not scared," he protested immediately.

She smirked. "Okay, maybe that's not quite the right word I should have used. I get that you're uneasy and that you don't want to cause trouble here within the family, but that doesn't have to happen."

"Well, if all goes well," he said, "it won't. But the minute there's any kind of an issue, you can bet I'll be the bad guy, and I'll have to find a new job. And I'm not really prepared to do that."

"Interesting," she said, with a nod. "I can see how that would work for you."

"But?" he challenged.

"Well, that doesn't really work for me anymore. I'll be going back to New York for a while. I may decide to come here to Africa on a permanent basis. I'm not sure yet. The bottom line is that you and I have unfinished business, and I would like to see where it goes." With that, she turned and headed toward the open doorway. "So I guess you have a decision to make."

"It's not like you're giving me any decision time," he said, swearing lightly.

"Since when do you need time to make this kind of a decision?" she asked, with a smile.

He shrugged, but he kept his hands in his pockets. Because he knew, if he moved them, he would grab her in his arms and hold her close.

She reached out her hand and said, "We could solve one thing right now."

"And what's that?" he asked, looking at her hand as if it was a viper.

She stepped forward again. "Whether there's anything to follow up on."

"That's not an answer," he said. "We already know something's there." He was deliberately holding back.

"And you also know," she said gently, "that we'll go up in flames the minute we take that step."

"So why would we do that?" he asked curiously.

She looked at him. "Are you for real?"

"Of course I'm for real," he said. "I don't like being mocked."

"I'm not mocking you," she said. "I guess I'm struggling with that sense of honor that's keeping you over there and me over here."

He struggled for a long moment and felt his inner resolve weakening. He closed his eyes and worked on his control, and, when he opened them again, she stood right in front of him, staring up expectantly. He could smell the fresh scent of her shampoo or whatever she used on her face. It was soft, feminine, and he could also sense the same pheromones he was struggling with. "Just because we want to doesn't mean it's something we should do," he said, as he fell back on the same old argument.

"No," she said, with a smile. "But it's something that's well past time." She wound her arms on his neck and pressed her long slim form against him. "Like I said, you have a decision to make."

"I can't make a decision when you're this close," he groaned.

"Good," she said. "That means you'll make the decision I want." And, with that, she stretched up on her tippy toes and kissed him.

CHAPTER 10

W HO KNEW IT would be so hard to get this man, who clung to his honor and his family life, the family he'd never had, to give up the tiniest little bit of control? But the minute her lips touched his, it was like an elastic band pulled too tight had snapped, and his arms anchored around her. She was lifted and slammed against the wall behind them, and she loved it; she reveled in each stroke of his hands, as if he couldn't get enough of her. His lips came down, hard and deep. Then he lifted her slightly and changed position, only to come down in a possessively drugging kiss that she'd never experienced before.

It took several moments before he finally gentled his body, pinning her in place, both of them needy and out of control. She moaned, as the passion ripped through her, sending her blood pressure boiling. She stretched up, wrapping her arms tightly around his neck, on her tiptoes, as she pressed hard against the ridge in his pants.

He pulled his head back, gasping for air. She dragged him back down again for another deep kiss. When he pulled back the next time, his voice was thick. "You're playing with fire."

"I don't care," she muttered. "Let's go now."

And in a move that she never would have expected from Fallon, he swooped down and picked her up. As if she were a small child, he carried her to the stairway. She kept kissing him, her hands moving over his body, his chest, and his cheeks. She'd been wanting to explore every inch of him for so damn long, she couldn't believe that finally they were there.

At her bedroom, she leaned over and opened up the door. As soon as they were inside, she slammed it behind them.

"Great way to let everybody else know," he muttered.

She searched his face, hoping he wasn't having second thoughts. "Quinn knows," she said gently.

He nodded. "Does anybody not know?"

"I don't know, and I don't care," she said. As soon as they got to her bed, he went to lay her down, but she wrapped her thighs around his hips, bringing him down with her.

He bowed his head against her forehead and said, "I need a moment to at least get my boots off."

She slowly released him, afraid that he would walk away from her, even now.

As she watched him kick off his boots, and his hands quickly stripped off his belt and jeans, she hopped to her feet and stripped off her own clothes, beating him in seconds.

He stared at her, his breath catching in the back of his throat, his gaze heated and dark. But she opened her arms, and he took a step forward into them.

She saw that he was warring with that part of him that had resisted for so long, and she shook her head and said, "No, come on. Now."

"Are you always so demanding?" he asked, with a quirk of his lips.

"If you even think about backing away right now," she

said. "You have no idea how much more demanding I'll become."

Muffled laughter escaped, but his lips were pressed tight against hers, so it was a sound more like a gargle between them. When their bodies came together, she felt the heat of his flesh; she shuddered and moaned, twisting sinuously against him, looking for every inch of contact she could get. They collapsed flat onto the bed atop the blankets, not having even a chance to pull them back. She wrapped her arms and thighs around him to hold him close.

He was already seated at the heart of her.

She wiggled beneath him, and he reared back and said, "Don't do that."

"Yeah," she said, with a smile. "Why not?"

He glared at her and slid his fingers into the curls at the apex of her thighs. She cried out, her hips rising against his fingers. "For the same reason you react to this," he muttered, lowering his head to kiss her navel. She twisted beneath him, her hands stroking his hair.

"You won't do too much of that either," she muttered.

"And yet," he said, "I've always believed in ladies first."

She groaned. "I just want you inside me," she pleaded.

"All in good time," he whispered.

"No. I've waited too long already."

He chuckled, but then her hand slid down, as she twisted to find him. When she grasped him in her long fingers, he groaned and shuddered, trying to pull away from her hand.

She shook her head and said, "Oh no, you don't."

At that, something snapped. He surged up, and she fell flat, her arms and thighs wide, accepting. In one plunge, he entered her right to the hilt.

She arched underneath him, crying out.

He went immediately still. "Oh God," he said. "Did I hurt you?"

"You'll hurt me now," she said, "if you don't finish what you started." She reached up and gently smacked him.

He chuckled and moved ever-so-slowly, but it was too damn slow for her. She lifted her hips up against him, again and again and again, as he plowed forward, the tempo getting faster and faster, until she collapsed back, completely overcome, her body taken through a tempest of a storm that he was in command of.

With sure footing, he drove her right to the edge and tossed her over, following right behind.

She remained underneath him, her arms holding his still-shuddering body, considering all these feelings. *Gladness, happiness, gratitude?* She wasn't even sure what she felt anymore; she was so overcome. To think that she'd waited this long, she buried her face against his neck and just hung on tight. He squeezed her gently and then shifted his position, so he wasn't quite on top of her.

She protested sleepily, but he shook his head. "I'm too heavy," he said, as he pulled her up tight against his side.

She snuggled in close, when he whispered, "Now will you sleep?"

She leaned up, kissed him gently, and said, "For a little bit and then I'll be back for more."

He groaned and said, "You'll kill me, if you are."

"As long as it's with happiness," she murmured and closed her eyes and slept.

FALLON CUDDLED THIS very special woman in his arms, realizing he had turned a corner. A corner he hadn't even seen coming. When he had first arrived, his mind had been completely focused on Bullard, and he hadn't even considered that Linny might have been here. And now? Now it was like his entire world had just shifted. He checked in with himself, checked in on the old programming, which he had used to keep his distance all these years. Then he thought about all the arguments she had used to get them here and how much courage it had taken her. It fit with what he knew of her.

He'd long admired the woman she had become, yet realized that he hadn't been the one to step up, to see that his program was old, and that it was time to change it. She had done that. It was an interesting thought. Would Dave really mind? Not if Fallon treated her well.

Dave had survived a heavy loss after his wife and daughter died, and he had adored his niece. She'd been very special to everybody. Would anybody else have an issue with this? Fallon realized that, even if anyone else did, it wasn't his problem. His job was to make sure that he looked after Linny as well as he could, regardless of the reactions of others. For the first time, he acknowledged that could mean changing jobs.

Not something he wanted to do because he really loved the team and the family here. This kind of explained why he had protested and had held out for so long, but, at the same time, it also made sense that the both of them were together. Now they'd taken that irrevocable step. It was what it was, and he couldn't change that.

Her hand patted his cheek. She murmured, "Stop thinking so loud."

He chuckled, pulled her closer, and whispered, "How can I not?"

"You're worrying," she murmured. "Let it be. It's all good."

He wasn't so sure he agreed with that, but he was willing to see where it went. "It could change everything," he said.

"Or it could change nothing," she whispered. She wrapped her arms tighter around him and, with a hug, said, "Trust in us."

At that, he realized that's really what it came down to. He had to trust that what they had was something special. That who they were together was something that would trump anything else. He had to decide where she appeared on his priority list, but he already knew. She came in at the top. As long as she had been on the back burner, he could carry on with everything else and think of her as being from another time, another place. But now that she was on the front burner, well, everything had shifted. She was now his priority. "I could get a job in New York," he said. He immediately felt her freeze in his arms.

Then she reared up over him, and she frowned at him. "Why the hell would you do that?"

He looked at her in surprise. "So the relationship can continue?"

"It can't continue here?"

"It's a little hard to carry on a relationship," he said quietly, "if you're over there, and I'm over here."

She sank back against his chest, as if realizing that he wasn't walking away from everything but trying to look at options, as to how to maintain the relationship.

"I am wondering about coming over here again," she said. "Like I said, Bullard sent me on this pathway, and he could sure use the help."

"He has talked in the past," he murmured, "about expanding the medical options here."

"Of course he would," she said, with a smile. "We'll see. I'm almost done."

"What does *almost* mean?"

"I think I've got four or five months left," she said, with a smile.

"That's not too bad," he said. "Then?"

"That's probably a couple missions for you." She smiled, snuggling in deeper. "Now can I go to sleep?"

He pulled her close, tucked her up against his heart, and said, "Sleep. I'll do the worrying."

"No worrying," she said. "Life isn't perfect, and you can't make it that way. We've made a decision to change something fundamentally important to who we are. Now we let the cards fall where they may, and we deal with the outcome." She yawned once and snuggled deeper and drifted off to sleep.

He smiled at her pragmatic and realistic answer. Because she was right. They had made a decision for all the right reasons, and, now that that decision was made, no way in hell he would change it. If people didn't like it, too damn bad. He's where he'd wanted to be all along. And, for that, he'd fight anybody who said it was the wrong thing. Closing his eyes, he too finally drifted off to sleep, after setting his internal alarm clock for thirty minutes.

CHAPTER 11

L INNY WOKE UP alone. She groaned at that and sat up, wincing at a twinge in her body, frowning at the absence of the closeness she had enjoyed earlier. She hoped what they had shared was enough to cement the decision in the brightness of daylight, where questions and doubts would linger. She'd really wanted to wake up with him, but, of course, it hadn't happened. She sat up, walked into the bathroom, and, as she washed, she looked at the shower and realized that's really where she wanted to be. Turning on the hot water, she stepped inside and braced herself against the wall, letting the hot water sluice over her body.

When she heard a voice call out in the bedroom, she said, "I'm in the shower."

The bathroom door opened, and he stepped in, holding a cup of coffee. She shut off the water, and he gave her a towel. She smiled, searching his face, but he didn't appear to have stepped back at all.

He looked at her in surprise. "What's with the look?"

"Just a little afraid that you would have second thoughts."

"Second thoughts about leaving the bed, yes," he said, with a nudge toward her damp body in the towel that she'd wrapped around herself, showing very interesting wet spots.

She smiled and said, "You can come back anytime."

"No," he said. "There's just so much still to deal with."

"Always so responsible," she teased.

His gaze was hooded. "Would that bother you?"

"I'll deal with it," she said easily. "We each have our own issues. As you will adapt to mine, I will adapt to yours."

He smiled at her. "It might not be that easy."

"It'll be as easy or as hard as we make it," she said, with a note of confidence that was real and driven from deep inside.

"If you say so."

She smiled and said, "Absolutely. Did you find out anything new?"

"No, but I've got a call to make to the police right now," he said.

"Good," she said. "I'll get dressed and come down."

"See you in a few minutes then."

As she stepped out into the bedroom to find clothes, she still didn't have very many options with her. If this would ever calm down, she wouldn't mind going shopping for a day and picking up a few outfits. Or, if it didn't happen, well, she was also okay with spending a lot of her days without much on, in bed with Fallon. But, as long as this strange stalker scenario here was going on, while the search for Bullard continued in the background, that wasn't likely to happen. Dressed again, she made her way down to the kitchen, where she refilled her cup of coffee and wandered into the control room.

Quinn looked up, flashed her a bright smile, and said, "Good morning again. You look well."

"I am," she said, with a cheery voice, and beamed at him.

He chuckled and winked at her.

She just grinned back.

Because Quinn and basically everybody else knew that only Fallon had been fighting so hard against their attraction, while the rest of the world wondered why he was taking his time. She understood, but now that it was taken care of, she felt a whole lot more secure about things.

She slipped up to Fallon and slid her arm around him, feeling him stiffen ever-so-slightly and then relax. "Did you make the call to the cops?"

"I did," he said. "It wasn't exactly helpful though."

"Did you give them the address of the warehouse?"

"They already had it, from Wagner I assume," he said.

"Great," she said, "and we still haven't any idea on that pimply face guy yet?"

"Nope, not yet," he said.

"Or any better understanding on that weird art?"

"Art is in the eye the beholder," he announced, and she chuckled.

"Good," she said. "Don't ever buy me anything like that then."

"I promise," he said. "It's an odd feeling to think of all those pictures of you up there on the walls too."

"Yeah, more creepiness than I care to deal with right now."

"Not a whole lot of choice," he said. "We have to deal with whatever comes up."

"Got it," she said. "But, so far, not a hell of a lot to go on."

"So often there isn't," he said, "until something trips them up."

"Is it this hard work that gets you where you are or that these criminals end up doing something stupid?"

"Both," Quinn said immediately. "If we're lucky, they

do something stupid early on, so that we can get a lead on them. In this case we're still trying to track down this guy with acne. And you would think that shouldn't be all that hard to do, but somehow nobody seems to know anything about him."

"Doesn't mean he's from this country at all," she said.

"No, it doesn't. He could be from the US or anywhere really."

She studied the picture they had set off to the side on one of the monitors. "I swear to God, I've never seen him before."

"And yet take a look at this," Quinn said, as he quickly ran the photo through some software program. Instantly it came up with different facial variations that completely changed the guy's face.

She gasped. "Oh, wow," she said. "That's ..." And she let her voice trail off because she didn't have any clue how to describe it. "When you do things like that, it's almost like he could be anybody."

"That's the problem," he said. "If he's any good at disguises, he *could* be anybody."

"But is that even likely? How many people know how to do things like this?"

"Well, if you just murdered somebody, what's the first thing you'll do?"

"Disappear," she said immediately.

"And, how will you disappear, if your name and face are found in photos, and that's how people know you?"

"Right, so you change your appearance," she said, as she nodded, looking at him.

"And that's just with a beard added. This one is just a hair dye, but each really makes a difference. And this one's got makeup on to cover all the acne," he said.

"And that makes a massive difference too," she admitted.

"*Great.*" On that note, she stepped a few paces away and said, "Technically we missed breakfast. I'll go make something to eat. Are you guys hungry?"

"I am," Quinn said.

"Me too," Fallon said. "I could use a meal."

"Coming right up," she said. She walked to the kitchen, wondering at the ease with which she had taken over things like the kitchen because of Uncle Dave. She'd often spent so much time in the kitchen with him because it had been a place where they could bond, a place where they could spend time together and just be themselves. It was time that she had thoroughly enjoyed spending with Uncle Dave over the years. It seemed odd to be here without him and kind of a unique experience.

Actually she had no doubt that her alone time with Fallon wouldn't have happened if Uncle Dave had been here. The reminder of that family duty, and the honor associated with it, would have been too much for Fallon to have broken. As it was, it had taken her to make that occur. She just hoped she hadn't pushed Fallon to compromise his sense of honor in a way that would somehow negatively impact things going forward.

Before long, she had a full-on smorgasbord of hoagie-style sandwiches, complete with side salads and baked beans. The men stepped into the kitchen, big grins on their faces.

"I sure love the fact that you're okay to cook," Fallon said. "A lot of women would have been upset at the idea of having to take up the slack."

"Cooking was how Uncle Dave and I always bonded when I was younger," she said. "So, if nothing else, it makes me feel closer to him right now."

"And I guess it doesn't happen very often, that he's not here when you are, does it?"

She smiled and shook her head. "No, it definitely doesn't."

At that moment, Uncle Dave called Fallon. He held up his phone and said, "Hey, Dave. I'm putting you on Speaker."

"Good," Dave said. "Are you guys okay?"

"We're fine," he said. "What about you?"

"I've got a little bit more brass to handle," he said. "So I'm off heading toward this third man. I'll probably be about four hours traveling, before I'll know for sure."

"Good enough," he said. "Don't give up hope. We'll find him."

"No, I won't," he said, "but it's damn discouraging. What about that weirdo?"

"Lots of weirdos at the moment. We're trying to find the little guy with acne you saw sitting in the car at the time."

"And I've racked my brain, but I can't give you any more details. I'm sorry."

"It is what it is. We've got images of him from the street cams," he said. "So we'll track him down."

"Right. Facial recognition is a good answer for that."

"We know. We're already on it."

He laughed. "Of course you are. Sorry, just me."

When he rang off, they looked at each other. "He does sound a little rattled, doesn't he?"

"Uncle Dave refuses to believe Bullard is not alive," she said. "I can't imagine how devastating it will be for him if it doesn't work out that way."

"Which is why we're not going there," Fallon said firmly.

"It doesn't change the probability factor," she warned.

"It is what it is," he said, using her words from earlier.

She smiled at him. "True. We'll deal with whatever we have to deal with."

He nodded. And just as he scooped more sandwiches onto his plate, his phone rang again. He looked down and said, "It's Wagner." He hit the button and said, "Hey. You're on Speakerphone."

"Wow, am I privileged or what?"

"Nope, you're interrupting a feeding frenzy," Linny said.

"Well, in that case, I won't disturb you too badly."

"Anything new?"

"Nope, other than this one guy is completely off."

"Well, we told you that in the first place," Fallon said.

"Indeed," Wagner agreed. "The bottom line at this point is that I'm not sure what our next move is. We've got a lot of forensic evidence. And it's pretty obvious that this group was an online forum and an art club. A couple are downtown," he said. "They appear to have a clientele very similar to this. I'll take a look and talk with a bunch of them today. Not sure if it will lead to anything, but, if others in the group bought those photos, it could help."

"Well, there are others," Quinn said, looking at Fallon.

Fallon just shrugged and nodded. "The one guy did give us some names. I'll email them to you," he said.

"Yeah, we'll run them, unless you guys did already."

"Yeah, we did, but we didn't get anywhere."

"Of course not. It's never that easy, is it?"

"Nope, it sure isn't."

When Fallon hung up again, she frowned and said, "You know I always thought it was. That easy, I mean. And I realize these missions are something that I don't have any experience with, but something always made me think it was easier than this."

"And yet it wasn't easy to track down your parents' killer either."

She nodded slowly, hating the reminder of how she'd become an orphan. Thank heavens for Uncle Dave's big heart. Her life would have been much different without him. "That's very true, just a weird thing all over."

"Sorry," he said. "It's still all legwork. It's all hard work to make things happen."

"Got it," she said. "I was just wondering if we could do anything else."

"Well, we have to track down everybody on that forum. But really what we want is the one guy."

When Fallon's phone rang for the third time, he just groaned and said, "If only they could leave me alone long enough to eat a sandwich." This time it was Ice. "Ice, hey, you got anything for us? You're on Speakerphone."

"Yes," she said, her voice musical and relaxed through the phone. "His name is Limerick. Jesse Limerick."

"Wow," he said. "How did you find that out?"

"Interpol," she said. "We have photos on the website."

"I checked there," Quinn said.

"Yeah, they were just pulled off a few months back," she said.

"And the photos?"

"They're pretty unclear, but it looks like him. We don't have any way to confirm, so we figured we'd toss that back to you guys, so you can do something."

"We got it from here, thanks," he said. "Jessie Limerick, right?"

"Yep. Let us know what you find." With that, she hung up.

"Now we just need an address."

But Quinn was already on it. "I've got two in town," he said.

She looked at him. "Two Jesse Limericks?"

"Yeah. A senior and a junior."

"Now that makes sense," she said, with a nod. "So, road trip?" She looked at Fallon.

He hesitated and then nodded. "Yep, road trip."

She grinned, then stood, walked around to kiss him gently on the cheek, and said, "You're learning." Then she walked out to get ready.

"SOUNDS LIKE YOU two have buried your differences," Quinn said. "I, for one, am happy for you."

"If it works out," he said. "I have to admit, I wasn't quite ready for the change."

"We're never ready for that kind of change," he said. "But you've got to be smart enough to grab it, when life gives you the opportunity to do so."

He nodded slowly. "I guess that's what this is all about, isn't it?"

"She's a good person, and it's obvious you do care about each other," he said. "Maybe, if you're lucky, it'll be your turn to make a success out of all this."

"I don't know," he said. "I don't really fit the pattern of everybody else in this chaotic world. And we've known each other for a long time."

"Sure, you have, but you haven't done anything about it," he said. "So I think it still counts. It's not like I've got a partner happening around here," he said, with a big grin.

"Maybe not," he said. "That doesn't mean it won't be your turn next."

He shrugged and said, "I'm not looking for that."

"But, if the opportunity drops into your lap …" he said, mimicking his friend's earlier comments.

At that, Quinn laughed hard. "So true." They quickly loaded the dishes into the dishwasher and checked on the weapons and ammo. By the time they were ready to walk out, as they laced up their boots, Linny came down the stairs, dressed and ready to go.

He looked her over quickly, nodded, and said, "Hopefully it'll be a quick trip."

"Hopefully it'll be a quick trip, *and* we grab the right guy," she said. "And we get this taken care of." Her voice was cheerful and calm.

He wondered at that, … how she sounded so calm. "You sound like you're totally okay with everything that's going on."

"I trust you guys," she said. "You'll do what you can to keep me safe, and, beyond that, it's out of everybody's control."

He nodded. "You can bet we'll do what we can. It hasn't failed us yet."

"I know," she said, with a gentle smile. "Let's go see who this pimple-faced person is and find out why the hell Interpol wants to know about him."

"Ice could send me the file," Fallon said.

Quinn said, "She didn't need to. I looked it up. He's been somehow involved in transporting illegal immigrants across Africa, into Europe, and eventually into England. Whether by land or by sea, Interpol is tracking that."

"Wow," she said. "Another stalwart citizen."

"Hardly, and surely not the mastermind," Fallon said, with a smile. "But that tends to be the level of people we're talking about."

"Right, so he's had lots of access to move around the countries."

"Exactly."

"But it still doesn't explain his obsession with these photos."

"Just because you don't like what they're calling art doesn't make it *not* art," Fallon said, laughing. He wrapped an arm around her shoulders as they walked to the vehicle. He stopped beside their multiple choices, looked at Quinn, and asked, "How dangerous do you think today will be?"

"Dangerous," he said cheerfully. "At least we're assuming. Let's take bulletproof, all the way."

With that, they chose one of the smaller trucks with bulletproof glass, one of Bullard's favorites.

"I forgot he spent so much money on his toys," she murmured, as she got into the middle of the seat.

"Some things that may appear to be toys are actually tools," Fallon said.

"Well, at least that's the excuse you gave yourself," she said, laughing.

"True. Besides," he said, "if it saves our lives, I'm all for it."

"Me too," she said. "Do we have an address?"

"I've got two of them," Quinn said, as he gave Fallon directions. Before long they pulled up in front of an address with raw acreage surrounding a run-down house.

She looked at it and frowned.

"Yeah, it doesn't look terribly appealing."

"Do you think somebody still lives here?" Linny asked. "It looks so derelict."

"Again, it's possible." Fallon shrugged.

"I've looked for a birthdate on senior but haven't got very much," Quinn added. "Just 1935."

"Well, definitely senior." Fallon laughed. "This could be his place, though he may not even still be alive."

"It's possible," Quinn said.

"So, given the age of the one guy," she said, frowning, "do we expect this to be a grandparent then?"

"That's what I was thinking," Fallon said. "Just because it's a senior and a junior, it doesn't tell you how old the junior is."

"Right."

They pulled up to the front door and parked, looking out the windows, watching for movement. Finally the guys shared a glance, then Fallon looked at her and said, "Please stay here."

She frowned and then nodded. "Fine. The house is probably empty anyway."

She settled back and watched as both men slipped out of the truck and headed to the front door. They knocked on the door, and, when there was no answer, the two men reached for the knob, as if to open it. She wondered at that. Quinn opened it and called out, asking if anybody was there. When they got no answer, or at least she presumed so, they stepped in. She frowned, hating to think of them going into somebody's place, but honestly it looked like nobody could even possibly live here. The windows were broken; paint was chipping, and it definitely looked like the roof had seen better days—like a decade ago.

She waited as the men searched inside, before they

stepped back outside again. When they did come out, she froze when she saw Fallon's face. She immediately hopped out of the cab of the truck and asked, "What's the matter?"

"Well, Doc, you want to come and take a look?"

"I won't like it, will I?"

"Not a whole lot, no," he said.

She walked over and followed him into the back of the house. "This place is nasty," she said.

"Yep," he agreed.

As they came around the corner, she saw a corpse on the floor. Not a recent corpse. Somebody who had died quite a while ago. She frowned, as she studied it. From where she was, it almost had a mummified look. "He's been gone for quite a while," she murmured, as she stepped closer.

"Yeah. And I don't see any visible cause of death."

"Not very easy to see in a lot of cases," she said. "Unless we're talking about a bullet hole or something obvious like that, which I'm not seeing any sign of."

"Exactly," he said. "It looks more like he died from natural causes. Or, looking at the condition of the body, I mean, maybe he starved? And he's on the floor. What are the chances that he fell and couldn't get up?"

"Good, unfortunately," she said. "That happens a lot in circumstances like this. An isolated house and, if he doesn't have anybody living close by, it could easily have happened that way."

As she studied the position of the body, she nodded. "I'm not in any way saying that is what happened, but it's definitely a possibility."

"So another phone call needs to be made."

"Yeah," she said, pulling out her phone.

As soon as she contacted Wagner, exasperation filled his

tone when he asked, "Another one?"

"Yes, another one," she said. "But hardly our fault. An old man. But we're searching for both a senior and a junior."

"Well, you didn't give me the ID of the man. Instead you headed off to check it out yourself."

At that, Fallon took the phone from her and said, "And, if we had sent you on a wild goose chase, you wouldn't have appreciated that either," he said. "We checked it out, and now we realize it needs your attention."

"Great," he said. "Do you have an address for the other guy too?"

"Yes, two addresses were in the phone book," he said. "We've checked this one, and now we're about to head out to check the second one."

"Well, you go do that," he said. "Let me know what you find." With that, he hung up.

They backtracked from the house, and she stood there for a long moment, staring.

"Are you okay?"

"I'm okay," she said. "But it's sad, you know?"

"You mean the fact that somebody lived and died here, and nobody knew? And that he could have been dead for months or even years?"

"Yes," she said. "Exactly that. Everybody should have somebody who will mourn them. Everybody should have somebody to be there with them on their last days."

"In a perfect world it would happen that way," he said. "But you and I both know, a lot is wrong with today's world, and looking after the elderly is just one more of those aspects."

Sad, she hopped into the truck, and they reversed down the driveway. "Wagner will come today, won't he?" she asked, twisting to look behind her.

"It really bothers you that he's there alone?"

"I guess in a way, yes," she said. "I don't think anybody should die alone, but, at the same time, I don't think a body should be there alone either."

"He'll be coming today," Quinn said. "We'll make sure of it."

She smiled at him and nodded. "I guess another day won't make a whole lot of difference, will it?"

He shook his head slowly. "Not to that guy anyway."

"I suppose this happens all the time, when you think about the world over."

"That it does. That it does."

With his mind churning with unanswered questions, Fallon drove to the second address. He couldn't imagine anybody not checking up on a senior member of the family like that. So, unless there were mitigating circumstances, like no family, maybe there was no connection between these guys, or maybe it was a relationship that had broken apart years ago. The old man had found himself in a tough spot at the end of the day. It was sad, like she'd said. But it wasn't the worst thing Fallon had seen in his life, that's for sure. He also didn't know just what this guy had been like when he was younger.

But, with nothing left to do but carry on, he drove steadily, following Quinn's directions. When Fallon pulled up outside a small apartment building, he said, "This makes more sense. It's similar to the apartment of the other guy."

"It is," Quinn said. "Not sure how much on the inside will match though."

"I don't like apartments," she said. "I've spent so much of my life in them, in some of the smallest accommodations because of the work I did and the hours I kept. So I didn't care that much at the time, but it's not what I would choose for my life."

"No, I don't think most of us would," Fallon said. "Me, I'm looking for a couple acres and a house in the middle, where I don't have to deal with people."

She laughed at that. "Yet you deal with a ton of people and live in a compound, where lots of people are around you all the time."

He just grinned.

As they hopped out, she asked, "Am I coming?"

He looked at Quinn and then at her and said, "You might as well. Let's see if he recognizes you."

"Right," she said. "That would be an interesting reaction to watch. Or not."

As they hopped out, it was midday but a Saturday. So hopefully he was home.

"If we found him," she said, "like, if this is him, which of course we don't know for sure, does that mean Interpol's not after him?"

"He was taken down off their site, so they could have him on a bail program or something like that, where he doesn't get to leave the country until he goes through a trial or something. It'll take a little more digging to get that kind of information."

"And did you notice that Wagner didn't offer us any-thing?"

"Wagner doesn't give us anything if he doesn't have to," Fallon said shortly. "I think it's the rule of these assholes."

She nodded. "Well, let's go see what we've got here."

Inside the building they moved toward the apartment in question. They had passed nobody on the way. Linny stepped up and knocked on the door. No answer. She looked back at Fallon.

He frowned and rapped on the door, harder. Checking his watch, "He shouldn't still be in bed."

"Says you," she said, with an eye roll.

He just shrugged, and, when he heard a shuffling sound inside, he stepped back slightly.

The door opened to show an older lady, quite elderly, standing in front of them. She looked up and winced. "Who are you?" she asked.

He confirmed the address and said, "We're looking for Jesse Limerick."

"My grandson," she said, with the nod of her head.

"Is he here?"

"Who's asking?" Something crafty was in her voice.

At that point, Fallon realized it wouldn't be quite so easy. "A friend of his has passed on," he said. "We were wondering if you had any information about it and the pictures."

She just rolled her eyes. "Those pictures," she said. "He's pretty addicted to them."

"Is he around? Could we talk to him about the pictures?"

She frowned and then said, "He hasn't been home for a couple days."

"Ah, does he have another place to stay?"

"No," she said. "I thought maybe he would have been with his grandpa, but they don't get along."

"So you don't live with your husband?"

"Haven't in years," she said. "Why?"

"Does his grandfather have the same name as him?"

She nodded. "Yep, he does. We raised him for years. His parents died, many, many, years ago. Now I live here with him."

"That's nice," he said. "Have you lived here with him for quite a while?"

She frowned and said, "You're asking an awful lot of questions."

"I am," Fallon said gently. "We were just at the grandfather's house."

"If you could even get in," she said. "That place is a pigsty."

"When did you last talk with him?"

"There you go, with the questions again," she said. "I don't talk to him. I haven't talked to him in a very long time."

"Ah," he said. "Then maybe you don't know."

"Know what?" she said, rubbing her eyes and staring up at him, her rheumy eyes almost teary, as if something was in them.

He suspected it was some eye condition. "We were just there this morning," Fallon said. "It appears that he passed away quite a while ago."

She just stared at him and blinked. "Who passed away?"

"Your ex-husband," he said, stepping forward.

The woman looked at him. "I told you. I haven't seen him in forever."

"Right, and is this the address of his house?" he asked, as he ran off the address.

She frowned and then nodded. "Yes, that's my old house. But I haven't lived with him for a long time," she reiterated once again.

"I see," he said gently. "Well, we went there and checked."

"Don't know why you'd want to do that," she said, with

a sneer. "It's not like he ever had anything to do with us."

"We found him deceased," Fallon said.

She looked at him and blinked. "You saying he's dead?"

"Yes," he said. "The police will be there now to take care of the body."

She looked at him in shock for a moment, then she started to laugh.

He winced. "I gather that news doesn't upset you."

"That's pretty funny actually," she said. "He always told me that I would die before him. Proved him wrong, didn't I." Then she started to hack and wheeze.

He stepped back in alarm, as she seemed to lose control.

Linny stepped forward and patted her gently on the back. "Maybe you should go lie down."

But the older woman brushed off her arm. "I'm fine. I'm totally fine." She shook her head. "Imagine that. The old coot's dead." She shook her head again.

"We're still looking for your grandson," Linny said. "Do you know where we could find him?"

"*Huh.* Why do you need to find him?"

Fallon thought about explaining it all over again with her, but Linny said, "We wanted to tell him in person that his grandfather was dead."

The woman looked at her, nodded, and said, "That makes sense. He should be downtown with his buddies."

"Do you know where that is?" Fallon asked.

"Where downtown is?" She looked at him, puzzled.

"Yes, but *where* downtown?" he asked, striving for patience.

"He likes to play pool," she said. "He's supposed to be getting a job, so he can pay for all the rent here that I pay for. He thinks I don't know about it, but I know he's not trying to find a job."

"Well, he's got a court case coming up, doesn't he?" Quinn asked.

She looked at him in surprise. "No, he's never been in trouble. Not my boy."

"Ah," he said, with a nod. "Good for you. You've done right by him."

"Of course I did. He's a good boy."

"Fine. We'll go down and tell him about his grandfather."

"He won't care," she said. "The last time he saw his grandfather, he beat him up pretty good." And she shuffled to shut the door.

"Okay, so the grandfather beat up the grandson?" Quinn asked Fallon, as they stepped out. "Or the grandson beat up the grandfather?"

"I don't think she was very clear herself," Fallon said.

But finding Junior in a pub with pool tables on Main Street in this tiny little town didn't sound too challenging.

"She didn't sound very upset about the death of her husband either," Linny said.

"Remember, in a perfect world …"

"I just struggle with all that," she said.

"Struggle all you want," he murmured. "Just remember. It's not that easy for people to change."

"I know." She smiled and slipped her fingers into his. "Glad you're in my life."

"Me too," he said.

"Hey, if you guys are getting all lovey-dovey," Quinn said, with a big grin on his face, "I'm leaving."

"*Huh*," she said. "You won't be leaving. Besides, take notes. Maybe you'll be next."

"I'm not next, no way," he said adamantly.

"I wouldn't put too much emphasis on that," she said. "Because, sure as hell, it's not something you can count on."

"No," he said. "Which is why I'm glad you guys finally got past your differences."

Back in the vehicle, Quinn ran down the local pub on his phone and loaded the GPS directions. They drove up toward town, choosing a parking spot a block away.

"Guess it'll be a little obvious if we all walk in there at once, won't it?" she asked the guys.

"I'm going around the back," Quinn said. "I bet Junior takes one look at her and pulls a runner."

"Wouldn't that be good," Fallon said, with a big grin.

"Why?" she asked.

"Because it shows guilt."

"No," she corrected. "It just shows he's afraid of the law. Although you don't look exactly like the law."

He just stared at her in surprise.

She shrugged and said, "Yet you're scary, so anybody in their right minds would run."

At that, Quinn burst out laughing and took off around to the back of the alleyway.

"I suppose we give him a few minutes, huh?" she asked.

"Yep, that's exactly what we'll give him," he said. "Then we go in and have a little talk with our guy, if he's here."

CHAPTER 12

LINNY AUTOMATICALLY STEPPED behind Fallon, as they walked into the door of the bar. He tried to usher her in front, but she chose to stay behind him. That way the shock of Junior seeing her would come up a little bit stronger, after Fallon had already broken the ice. As they walked in, the bar was shadowy and dark. A typical pub pool parlor, as far as she was concerned. Particularly in this part of town, which would never be a high-class area. As they walked in, nobody even looked up or gave a shit.

About six guys were in the place, only one at the pool table. The others weren't even hanging around, so if that was the guy they were looking for, he was playing pool by himself. As she and Fallon walked up closer, she peeked around Fallon and realized it could be him. He was fairly small, and his face was definitely covered in pimples.

"Jesse Limerick?" Fallon asked.

The guy at the pool table froze, and she watched as he shook his head and said, "He's not here today."

He didn't react to seeing her. She wondered about that.

"What the fuck, man," said one of the other guys from the counter. "You're Jesse."

"I am not," he said, as he turned to Fallon and added, "What can I help you with?"

"We're looking for Jesse Limerick," he said. "It's something to do with his grandfather."

At that, the kid stopped and stared. "What about my grandfather?"

"So you are Jesse Limerick?"

The other guy up at the counter laughed and laughed.

Jesse turned and said to him, "Shut the hell up." Then he faced Fallon. "What about my grandfather?"

"He's dead," Fallon said easily.

The kid looked at him in shock, and then he started to laugh. "Well, maybe I can finally move my grandmother out of my place then. Jesus Christ, living with her is a pain in the ass. I moved here to get away from her."

"Yet apparently she pays all your bills," he said, raising an eyebrow.

"That's a damn lie," he sneered. "And she's a pain in the ass. Now she can move back home again."

"She says that she hasn't lived there for years."

"Not for about six months or so," he said. "Don't know if it's been even as long as that."

"Not according to what she said," Fallon said, his voice cautious.

"It doesn't matter what she says. She's loopy in the head. She stays with me, so I make sure she gets some food in her. Otherwise she'll not eat for days. So what happened to him?"

"We don't know. He's been dead for a while."

"Of course he was. That figures. If he died alone, I'm all for it. He was a mean old bastard."

"So, no love lost there, huh?"

"Nope, not at all. Last time I saw him, we had a hell of a fight."

"Did you hit him, and then he hit you?"

"Who gives a shit," he said. "By the end of it, we were

both hitting each other. It was years ago. I wouldn't have had anything to do with even my grandmother, but she arrived on my doorstep, looking for help. What the hell was I supposed to do?"

"Well, it's a good thing that you did help her," he said. "Obviously she might need help through this trying period as well."

"Not likely," he said. "Those two, they never got along."

As they headed back to Ben's apartment building, based on a tip Jesse gave them, she glanced at Fallon, still surprised and somehow warmed on the inside that she was with him. She tossed him a special smile, seeing a fire light up the dark depths of those wonderful eyes.

Quinn was driving, which was a damn good thing, given the charged atmosphere. Fallon shifted slightly and turned his attention to his phone and the GPS.

"Do you think Jesse is the same guy that Ice found on Interpol?" she asked.

"If he is, he's a good actor."

"Doesn't mean that he, in his own weird way, wasn't just telling the truth as he saw it," Quinn said. "We've seen guys like that too."

"Doesn't make me feel any better," she muttered. "Feels like we have more going on than ever, and it's hard to sort out the origins of these issues."

"That's fairly typical, when we track down people and crimes. These other threads get caught up in our net, so we have to solve them or weed them out, yet stay on our target and not get sidetracked," he said. "Now Jesse pointed us to Keith and John, wherever he is, but both those names were written on the back of the photos on Ben's door. Hopefully Keith can lead us to a John in the same building. From there, who knows? Does any of this lead us to finding who sabotaged Bullard's plane? I hope so, but, to date, that answer eludes us."

They hit Ben's apartment building again, with all of them getting out and locking up the vehicle. Back upstairs at the apartment where Ben had stayed, Fallon stopped and said, "So this is Ben's apartment, and up several floors is the idiot Keith, but Limerick is saying that somewhere in between the two of them, is where this other guy John lived?"

"Do we trust Limerick though?" Quinn asked. "Think about that. We don't have anything other than Limerick's word for it."

"And I wouldn't trust him at all," she said.

"So what are we doing, starting with Keith, the same guy upstairs?" Quinn asked.

"If he's even alive," she muttered.

Quinn shot her a sharp glance. "Why would you say that?"

"Because a lot of people end up dead. It's like they're turning on each other and don't care what the tale is."

"That's what happens when rats get cornered," Fallon murmured. "Let's start with the neighbor lady. She may have more info. We just won't tell her that Ben's dead." They walked down to the apartment of the lady Quinn had spoken to yesterday.

Linny knocked here and, when the woman answered, Linny smiled at her and said, "Hi, we're looking for that friend of yours again, Ben, or John maybe?"

She looked out and saw Quinn. Immediately she fluffed up her hair and said, "Hey, handsome."

He smiled at her and asked, "Hey, have you seen Ben

lately?"

"Nope, sure haven't seen that loser," she said, with a sneer.

"Have you seen anybody else around here, like John or Keith?" Linny asked.

"No," she said. "Place has been dead as a doorknob."

"So you haven't seen Keith come or go at all?"

"No."

At that, Fallon stiffened. Because that could possibly mean something completely different than what they wanted. They all smiled and thanked her.

The woman headed back inside her apartment, then she turned and asked, "You're the girl, aren't you?"

"Yes," Linny said, without any argument. "I certainly am. But not by choice."

"Good," she said. "You don't want to get mixed up with none of that photography stuff. That turns bad, fast."

"Well, they did it without my permission," she said, murmuring to herself as she walked away. She didn't want anybody thinking that she'd been a willing part of this, but somehow just having her face all over the door or walls was likely to do that.

They all headed up to the sixth floor to return to Keith's penthouse apartment. As they got to his apartment, she watched as Fallon quickly unlocked the door and stepped inside. Quinn stayed out in the hall with her.

"Shouldn't we go in?" she asked, surprised that they remained in the hallway.

"Well, it's probably a good idea," he said. "But first we'll wait to make sure it's clear."

She frowned. "Meaning?"

He motioned at the open door where Fallon stood. He

turned to her as he had heard the entire conversation.

"I'm checking to see if Keith's here," Fallon said. He turned and strode down through the entry hallway in this apartment. As he walked from room to room, it seemed like the place was completely empty. He saw the suitcases that the guy had been trying to run away with, when they'd talked to him before, and they didn't appear to have been opened or disturbed in any way. He frowned at that and then turned to look back at Quinn. Fallon did a full search through the place but found nothing.

When he came back to them, he said, "Nothing's different from when we were here last time. The suitcases are still packed, but Keith's not here." He said all of that, with emphasis. He looked at her and said, "Meaning, he's not dead inside his apartment."

Relief washed over her face. "Well, I'm glad to hear that," she said, "because that's pretty irritating to think that would be the killer's next solution."

"It's not a solution," he said, "but it's definitely something we have to look at."

"So I suggest we go downstairs," Quinn said. "Just make sure that Ben's apartment is still the same."

"The cops have been in there by now, haven't they?" she asked.

"Don't know," Fallon said. "Let's go find out." They trooped back downstairs, and, even as she walked out on Ben's floor, she turned to look back at the woman's door. But it was closed.

Fallon looked at it. "Anything wrong?"

She just shrugged. "There's a lot wrong," she said. "Just nothing I can pinpoint."

"Well, we know the feeling," he muttered, looping his

arm with hers.

"When people get like this," she said, "it's hard to even imagine how some of this stuff came about."

"It is," Fallon agreed. "On the other hand, we'll get to the bottom of it."

She nodded and said, "Every step, we're getting a little closer."

"That's how these puzzles work."

At Ben's apartment, Fallon found it locked, but no crime scene tape was affixed or anything to say that they weren't allowed to enter. Of course it was a locked apartment, so, in theory, they weren't allowed to enter at all. He looked at Quinn who quickly stepped forward and picked the lock, letting them in. As soon as they opened the door, they both reared back.

She closed her eyes and groaned. "Okay, so another dead body," she said. "Who will volunteer to go see which one it is?"

"I will," Quinn said, as he stepped forward. He returned a moment later.

Her fingers tightly clenched Fallon's. She tried to ease back her grip, but he just gave her hand a reassuring squeeze. She looked at Quinn. "Who is it?"

"Keith. Our guy from upstairs, with his luggage all packed," he said heavily. "Looks like he took five to the chest, with heavier ammunition. In fact, most of his chest was just blown apart."

"Wow," she said. "So he came down here to do what?"

"Rob the photos in this place most likely," Quinn said. He turned to look around. "I don't see anything different, except for the addition of a body," he said.

"Interesting," she murmured. "So he just came in because we told him Ben was dead or what?"

"It's hard to say," he said. "We'll have to let Wagner know."

She groaned and said, "Well, somebody else is contacting him this time. He won't take my calls anymore, after all this."

The two men smiled at her.

"Get used to it," Quinn said cheerfully. "At one point in time or another, these guys don't like any of our calls."

She smiled. "You know what? I'm starting to realize why," she joked. Something about having that bit of humor to play with made it a whole lot easier to be here.

Sure enough, Quinn pulled out his phone and called Wagner to report yet another death. She heard the disgust in Wagner's voice on the other end of the phone, as Quinn held up his phone for them.

"We don't do this on purpose," she added into the phone.

"Is that you, Linny?" he asked. "You should know better than to hang around with these guys."

"I've been hanging around with them for a lot of years," she muttered.

"I'm coming," he said. "Would you just get out of everybody's apartment?"

"Well, we could," Fallon said, "providing you guys were actually doing your job."

At that, Wagner's voice hardened. "I should charge you for breaking and entering."

"Or you could reward us," she said. "For making a welfare call, out of concern for a person who's been missing."

He stopped at that and said, "Whatever." Then he hung up on them.

Quinn looked at Fallon. "Wow, we're making friends every time we turn around."

"Do you guys have friends?" she asked curiously. Both men just glared at her, and she started to laugh.

"See? Humor makes it easier, doesn't it?" Fallon whispered.

She nodded. "It's a little hard to realize that, every time we turn around, we're coming across a dead body."

"It's not getting us the answers we need," he said. "Somebody is ahead of us."

"There always is, and that's what's frustrating," she said. "Who else is even involved in this, and why?"

"That's what we have to figure out." Fallon sighed.

She shook her head. "Are you sure you don't want to go in and take a quick glance around?"

"Oh, I will," he said, as he looked at Quinn. "I'll be back in a moment." Fallon turned to her. "You want to come in?"

"Not particularly," she said. "I've seen my share of dead bodies in my world."

"Of course," he said, as he stepped in.

She looked at Quinn. "Do you think I should go in?"

"Only if you think we might have missed something, or you might recognize something specifically from last time."

"Not particularly," she said. "Wasn't it a mess before?"

"Yes, and nothing's really changed," he said, giving her that half smile.

She nodded. "It all sucks."

Just then Fallon stepped back out again and looked at her. "Last chance."

She groaned and said, "Well, I should, I guess." And, with him at her side, she stepped forward and walked through the small apartment. As she got deeper inside, she said, "I wish I understood what if anything this had to do with me."

"Well, Ben's body was found outside your compound."

"And yours and yours," she said, as they walked out to join Quinn.

"That's true, and that's something that hopefully we can link them to, when we get there."

"Maybe, but, at the moment, we don't really have a whole lot to go on."

"Except that we're under watch," he said. "As we know from Paris, everybody is watching us, even when you think they're not."

"Creepy," she muttered.

They walked back outside the building to wait for Wagner to arrive. When he did, he looked at them, frowned, and said, "Are you three done causing trouble?"

"Do you want us to show you or not?" Fallon asked.

"Yes," he said. "Lead the way. After all, you guys are apparently law enforcement around here."

So much sarcasm filled his tone that it was all she could do to not laugh. She looked up at Quinn. "I'll stay out here with you, if you don't mind."

"Absolutely," he said, as they both watched the two men head inside the apartment building.

"Doesn't Wagner look thrilled," she murmured.

"He always looks that way because this just adds more work to his plate."

"So aren't we solving some of these problems for him?"

"I don't think he considers it a good trade-off."

"Of course not," she muttered, as she walked around in a small circle, easing the strain on her neck.

"Is that a tension headache?"

"Absolutely," she said. Just then a vehicle drove by very slowly.

He said, "Don't look now, but we're being watched."

She froze. "How do you not look?" she muttered. "I mean, I instinctively want to turn around and take pictures."

"Not going to work," he said. "It's gone."

"It doesn't matter that somebody did that?"

"It's hard to say. But they slowed down, as they came upon us out here."

"Great," she muttered. "Is that related to you or to this mess? Or maybe they just saw Wagner's vehicle here."

"Always and again, a lot of options."

"And none are giving us any answers," she noted.

"Nope, answers are one of those things we have to work for."

Just then they heard somebody walking down the street. As the footsteps came around the corner, she recognized Jesse from the pool hall. "Wow, look at that," she said to him. "Fancy seeing you here."

"What?" he said. "I was just coming to talk to Keith. To see if you guys figured out what he was up to."

"Interesting," she murmured. "We don't exactly have anybody to talk to."

"Besides," Quinn added, "the cops took him in for questioning."

At that she froze, looked back at Quinn, and frowned. He just gave her a gentle nudge, and she realized that nobody had asked when Keith had been released from the police interview, pinpointing what time he had gone home. Had he come straight home or gone straight to Ben's apartment?

She looked at the pool player and said, "Besides, what do you care? You said he wasn't even a friend."

"The whole group of them were just weird," he said.

"So that makes you weird by association, doesn't it?"

"Hell no," he said. "I'm not one of them."

She nodded slowly. "Well, they're all dying like flies," she said. "So maybe that's a good thing. Unless of course you've got anything to do with it."

He glared at her and said, "You got no cause to even say that to me."

"I can say what I want," she said smoothly. "Until you've proven your innocence."

"Could have been you who killed him," he stated. "I mean, I kind of like that idea. Maybe you were jealous that he wasn't paying you the royalties for your photos."

"Oh, so you did recognize me," she said, with a smirk. "In the bar it looked like you were trying so hard to not let on that you knew who I was."

"Well, if you think you're some kind of a celebrity, you're wrong," he snapped. "This guy, and what he was doing to those photos, should have made you very wary."

"In what way?" Quinn asked curiously.

"In the sense that his mind was obviously not fully there. How long before his affections went from photographs to wanting actual flesh-and-blood?"

A chill washed over her shoulders as she studied him. "Or how long before anybody who was collecting those photographs," she murmured, "would have the same transference issues."

He looked at her, smiled, and nodded. "Right, lots of guys have those photographs," he said. "So how well do you sleep at night?" Then he started to whistle as he turned and walked away.

FALLON AND WAGNER only heard the last part, as they came out the front door, just in time to realize who Linny and Quinn were talking to, with the barbs slinging back and forth.

"Interesting that he came by," Fallon muttered.

"And who's that one?" Wagner asked.

"Somebody you need to talk to."

"And speaking of talking to you," Linny said, looking at Wagner. "When did you guys let that guy Keith go from the police station?"

"We only kept him for a few hours of questioning. He was supposed to come back today."

"Well, I guess he didn't make his appointment then, did he?"

He glared at her. "Not my fault," he said. "We didn't have any reason to keep him."

"Well, how about for a mental exam?" she muttered.

"Just because he was unstable doesn't mean that we can just hold him. He must be a danger to himself or others."

"Well, whatever he was doing," she said, "it's got nothing to do with Bullard at least."

"Says you," Wagner replied.

"Why would you say that?" she asked, slowly turning to look at him.

"Because we did find something on this Keith person."

She looked at Fallon, surprised. "What did you find?" she asked Wagner.

His tone was grim, as he said, "A message." He looked at Quinn. "You wouldn't have seen it if you just checked his pockets. But a message was written on his arm, in permanent ink."

"I'm scared to ask," Quinn said, wincing. "What's the

message?"

"*Just because he's gone, doesn't mean you're safe.* Besides those words was the Kingdom Securities logo."

They stared at each other.

She asked Fallon, "Is that a message about Bullard?"

"You can't assume that," Wagner said.

"Like hell we can't," Fallon said. "So who the hell in our circles would have any clue about these guys? Are they just getting us all stirred up as part of their fun?"

"It's possible," Wagner said. "We don't have any answers yet."

"We never have any answers." She turned and stormed back toward the vehicle.

Quinn looked at Fallon. "No other IDs, no tattoos?" he asked.

Fallon shook his head. "Just the logo, from Kingdom Securities."

"Shit," Quinn said. "So we're back to that again?"

"Looks like it," Fallon replied. "Deedee's rogue guys are still out there, and, now that she's dead, nobody's got a handle on them at all."

"So why did we come over to Africa? Maybe we should have stayed over there in Paris."

"We're over here because obviously they're here too," he reminded Quinn.

Quinn shook his head. Just then a vehicle caught his attention. A black truck.

Fallon followed his gaze as it approached and said, "Have you seen that truck before?"

Quinn said, "Yeah. It came by a few minutes ago, driving slow."

When it got up beside them, weapons were suddenly

shoved out the windows, and gunshots ripped through the air.

CHAPTER 13

L
INNY SCREAMED AS gunfire filled the air. But she was tackled from the side, as Fallon threw her to the ground behind their vehicle. Fallon held her close.

As soon as the gunfire ended, the vehicle ripped away and took off.

"What a little bastard," she said, trying to sit up. But Fallon wouldn't let her go. "Are you hurt?" she asked, turning around to look at him.

He sat up grimly. "It's just a graze." Sure enough, he'd taken a bullet across his arm, enough to split the skin and to burn the flesh underneath.

She gasped, as she immediately looked for something to staunch the bleeding.

"It's fine," he said, as he called out, "Quinn?"

"Yeah, I'm okay," he said. "I took a little nick, but that's all."

"Me too," Fallon replied. "Wagner, what about you?"

Silence.

Fallon bolted to his feet, and she came flying after him, racing toward the fallen man. As they approached, she gasped and fell to her knees, "Oh! Oh, my God. Oh, my God."

Wagner was on the ground, bleeding from an ugly shoulder wound. They kept pressure on it to slow the bleeding.

"Oh, my God," she kept saying. Then she gave herself a hard shake. "Was this meant for Wagner?"

"I don't think so," Quinn said. "I was standing right beside him. Something caught my eye on the ground, and I'd bent down, thinking it might be a key when the shooting started. So I've got a graze on my arm, but I missed getting hit."

They stared at each other, as they all realized just how close a call that had been.

"Okay, things are getting seriously ugly here," she muttered, as she looked down at Wagner. "I feel really sad for him."

"I'll be fine," Wagner snapped. "Just resting, with my eyes closed. Don't count me out yet."

"It's also the work he does," Fallon said. "Normally we would say this investigation would be pretty easy, but obviously it's gotten a whole lot worse right now."

She looked up at him. "Do you think it has something to do with the message?"

"I would think so," Fallon said. "We didn't look to see if the door was triggered."

"No, because it looked like the police had already been and gone," Quinn muttered. They bent down, studying Wagner.

"We'll have to call this in," Quinn said, standing up and stepping away from them. "Give me a minute to make the calls."

As Fallon tried to pull her back to the safety of the vehicle, she said, "No, I'm not leaving him here like this."

"That's fine. We can stay here as long as that vehicle doesn't come back," he said. "We're sitting ducks out here."

"I hear you," she said, "but Wagner's here because of us."

Fallon hugged her tight against him, as he whispered, "I know. I know that. But we can't be blamed for all this. I'm sorry you had to see that, but this kind of stuff is what makes our world so ugly."

"It sucks," she muttered. She gave him a hard hug and then turned to look at him and said, "So how do we make this a whole lot less dangerous for everybody around us?"

"Take it away from the public," he said immediately. "Imagine if somebody had come out of that apartment building?" Even now, people were peering through windows and doors, just to see if it was safe. Some ventured out the front door. Fallon smiled and said, "Look at them. They're all coming out to see if it's okay."

"Curiosity?"

"To a certain extent, but also just the fact that an awful lot of noise was out here. They want to know what was happening."

"Understood," she muttered.

Quinn came back moments later. "Cops are on the way," he said.

"Is that a good thing?" she asked.

"It's not a bad thing," he said. "Also called Wagner's office, and they're leading this attack now."

"And the message on Keith's arm?"

"I'm not certain about the meaning of that. However, you can get ready for some pretty intensive questioning," Quinn said quietly. "It's one thing for them to have Wagner handling all this. It's another thing completely when somebody went after Wagner himself."

"Is that what we think happened?" she said.

"I don't know, but what I can tell you," he said, "is that the next couple hours will be intense."

TO SAY IT was intense was to put it mildly. Once Wagner's team arrived, things were taken completely out of their control. Fallon saw a certain amount of calming on Linny's part, once the professionals stepped in. Though he didn't want to give her a false sense of security over something like this because the gunmen could just as easily have been one or more of Wagner's teammates. But Fallon didn't want to consider that either.

By the time they had finished with all the questions, she looked absolutely exhausted and heartsick. Then they were finally released. It was well into the afternoon, and they'd seen several of the locals coming and going, trying to get details and answers. The whole time a large circle of curiosity-seekers surrounded them.

By the time they finally loaded up into their vehicle and left, Fallon said, "I think everybody and their dog was out there."

"I saw the woman we spoke with out there too," Linny muttered. "It's not surprising that she would want to know what happened. What I wonder is whether she had any part in it. I wanted to walk over and say something to her but figured it was better off if I didn't."

"You don't know how she would have reacted."

"She also probably doesn't know about her friend Ben being dead."

"Right."

"Still, I feel so sad for Wagner. I know his wound's not as bad as it was bloody, but still he'll need a few days to recover."

Fallon did too, but this wasn't the time to deal with it.

"I contacted Ice as well," Quinn said.

"Well, it's not all one issue," she murmured. "Obviously we have something else mixed into this."

"Actually," Fallon said, his tone dark, "I think someone was using more vulnerable members of society to make their agenda happen."

Quinn looked at him, even though he was driving, and said, "You want to elaborate?"

But she jumped in and said, "That's actually a good idea. I mean, I hate to say it, but it's, you know, from a killer's perspective, probably a good idea."

"Yes," Fallon murmured. "But it leaves people vulnerable here who could later expose you."

"Right."

At that, Quinn pulled off to the side of the road and said, "Okay, English, please."

"Not a whole lot to say," Fallon said. "Just that we think somebody was using people from this chat group, who all lived in a certain area near here and who all had a connection to the compound. Who knows how he found out about that connection, but anybody who saw these pictures would know, right? But they used the art forum nuts to get to us. They used these guys as pawns, then took them out one by one, cleaning up behind them without a care, in order to get to us."

"Yet why would you take out all these people just to send a message? Why not come to the compound and completely annihilate us?" she asked.

"She's right. Has to be another reason in there," Quinn said.

"Maybe somebody was doing a quid pro quo," Fallon muttered.

Quinn nodded slowly. "That would make sense. You get rid of this person because that's what I want, and I'll do the same for you."

"But who's connected to all this?" she asked. "Who would do something like that?"

"Now that is what we don't know," Fallon muttered.

CHAPTER 14

A S SOON AS they got home, Linny needed something to do to keep her busy and decided on making an early dinner. She went to the fridge and pulled out the steaks she'd planned on cooking tonight. She looked at the men and said, "Anybody up for barbecue?"

"That sounds like a good idea," he said. "We'll go check security."

She nodded and said, "I'll season these and let them sit for a while and get a big salad ready. Then I'm heading for the pool. If there's one thing I need right now, it's a little stress relief."

"Got it," Fallon said. "You go do that."

She headed back to the kitchen, seasoned the steaks, and threw together a salad, trying to focus only on the pool that waited for her. She went up to her room and quickly changed into her bathing suit. Grabbing her towel, she headed down to the pool, spread her towel over a lawn chair, and, standing at the edge of the cold clear water, she dove right in.

This is what she needed. As soon as the water crashed over her head, she felt some of the stress coming off her shoulders. Immediately she broke through the surface and started out with a steady front crawl. She swam one length and then another. And then back and forth again. Such coiled-up tension ran through her that she needed an outlet of some kind.

She expected the men to join her as soon as they were done with their security checks, whatever that meant in this case. She had a good idea of how the place ran, but she wasn't up on all the latest things that they had to work on. And it was still a crazy system they had. It was intense, with a lot of monitors. She needed to learn it, just as she had learned the previous one.

When she finally came to a stop, she pulled herself out of the water and sat here, her back to the house, just studying her surroundings, spending a few minutes trying to enjoy the Zen backyard space that Uncle Dave had worked so hard on. Bullard had designed a lot of it, and Uncle Dave continuously improved it. Her uncle was really talented, and he had spent a lot of his life here, so it was home for him. She couldn't imagine him ever leaving.

Then, with a pang, she thought about herself ever leaving it too. Change was hard, and change like this was even more brutal. She stretched, stood, and walked to a patch of sunlight, where she did several yoga moves to slow down the rest of the stress eating away at her.

By the time she was done, she walked to the lawn chair, stretched out, and closed her eyes. A little bit of a nap could never hurt, especially with all that had gone on over the last few days. Soon she drifted in and out of sleep. She heard somebody come out and check on her, mumbled to him, then rolled over and went back to sleep again. When she woke the next time from her power nap, she felt a whole lot better.

She sat up, stretched again, and walked back to the kitchen. The steaks sat where she'd left them, and, for that matter, everything else had been left as is too. She walked to the fridge to see if the guys had put any beer in. Normally they kept it full and cold, but the last few days had been anything but normal. Not hearing anything, she walked into the command center and found no one there. She kept on going throughout the house, looking for the men. Only as she went back upstairs to their rooms did she get seriously worried.

She grabbed her phone from the pocket of her coverup and sent Fallon a text. **Where are you?**

When she got no answer, she felt her blood run cold. The compound was huge, but did somebody get in while she was sleeping? Just the thought made her cringe, to think that somebody might have seen her in the pool, or even worse, while she'd been stretched out asleep on the lawn chair. But she saw absolutely nothing to confirm a stranger was here or that the men had left.

She quickly raced to the garage, but all the vehicles were still there. Slowly she walked back to the kitchen and then outside to the lawn chair, where she had been, and started fresh. From there she followed back to where the men had said they would be, then she texted everybody she knew, but nobody had heard from the men. She went back up to her bedroom, quickly changed, again came back downstairs, wondering what her options were. Because the way it looked now, she was alone and on her own because Fallon and Quinn were missing.

Had they been taken?

They wouldn't have left her behind intentionally. She remembered somebody coming out while she slept by the pool, but surely the guys wouldn't have left without her?

In her heart of hearts, she didn't believe that Fallon

would have left her voluntarily. Deciding to give the place a complete sweep, searching every closet and every floor, she started in the basement and worked her way up. When she circled around to the garage, stepping inside, she saw a chain wrapped around one of the floor-to-ceiling cupboards and frowned. She headed over and, using a pry bar, with great difficulty managed to snap the chain.

As soon as she did, the double doors opened, and a man she'd never seen before crashed out. She stared at him in shock, automatically bending to see if he was alive. Not only was he not alive, but also he was recently dead if the pool of blood inside the cupboard was anything to go by. Blood was all over him, as if he had taken a heavy blow and then had been immediately locked up. He was still warm too. But then, hell, she hadn't been asleep very long either. This now changed the entire game.

She quickly took a picture of the guy's face and sent it to Ice, with a text message. **He's dead.**

Ice phoned a moment later and said, "Do you have a place you can lock yourself in?"

"I don't know," she said. "But I'm sure as hell not doing that if Fallon and Quinn are here somewhere and hurt."

"I get it," she said. "But, if you get hurt, that won't help anybody."

"None of this is helping us," she said. "The last I heard, they would check on the security. I went to the pool, swam a few laps, and then I crashed, took a short nap."

"Then all hell broke loose while you were out. I got it," she said. "That's the way the other end likes to work."

"Meaning?"

"Meaning, that somebody waited for the perfect oppor-tunity and probably jumped one of our guys, then the other."

"And left me there, sleeping?"

"Don't take this the wrong way," Ice said apologetically, "but they probably didn't think that you were much of a threat."

She gave a stark cry at that. "Then I need to find him," she said fiercely. "I'm not losing Fallon, now that I'm finally with him."

A strangled note came from Ice. "*With him?*"

"We've been dancing around this for years, and now we're together," she added fiercely. "I'm not losing that."

"I get it," she said. "We've got men coming toward you."

"Doesn't matter if they are or they're not," she said. "They'll be walking into a trap."

"And you have to expect that," she said. "Whatever is going on right now, they have probably got whoever it is, still there, waiting for you to do something, playing with you."

"Or maybe they took off with the guys."

"Check the video feed," Ice urged.

At that, she raced back to the monitors and said, "I tried earlier, but I couldn't see anything. They upgraded the system while I was gone last time."

"It's the same system we've got," Ice said, and then she led Linny through it.

When she finally got the monitors up, Linny said, "They stopped the video feed when we came home."

"In that case, I believe somebody was already inside the compound."

"Then what? They completely wiped out the monitors?"

"No, they probably left some parts of it operational, for whatever reason. I don't know."

"Just to torment the guys, I suppose."

Linny quickly filled in Ice on the message they had found on Keith's arm too.

"That makes sense. Somebody's playing them."

"But why? That's not normal."

"These games are all about superiority, about who's the best," she said, fatigue evident in her voice. "So, once the shake-up happened with Bullard's flight," she said, "there's been a fight in the rest of the world as to who'll take his place."

"And what if he's not dead?" she said fiercely. "He's like another uncle to me."

"I know he is," Ice said. "He's important to me too, and his half-brother is devastated. But that doesn't change the fact that, until we know more, we have to assume that, if Bullard's alive, he's either in a very bad state or we would have heard from him."

No refuting that logic. "So what do I do right now?" she asked, staring around. "God, this place is giving me the creeps."

"That's only because you're alone, and it feels like you're under attack," she said. "I'll assume that you are. Which is why I want you to find a place to go hole up and to stay hidden."

"I told you," she said. "I'm not doing that." Just then, as she walked through to the kitchen, she thought she heard a heavy sound. "I heard something," she whispered.

"Hide," Ice said immediately.

Not too many places to hide, but she was beside the pantry, so she slipped inside and crawled underneath the very large shelves on the bottom. Pulling herself in and trying to be as tiny as she could, she waited. With Ice on the phone, just then Linny heard voices. "Somebody's here," she whispered.

"Be quiet," Ice said. "Keep the phone turned toward the voices, so I can hear." With that, they listened to the sounds of a man outside.

"She's got to be here somewhere," he said. "What do you mean?"

She realized he was talking to somebody on the phone.

"Well, she was sleeping outside, when I left her. I don't know where she is now. She's got to be here. ... Yeah, yeah, yeah, I've got them locked up. ... No, not a problem. And, yes, I've got her too."

At that, she gasped. She heard Ice quietly say, "Calm down. This is too important."

Linny just nodded.

"No, no, I know. I've picked her up. She wasn't very cooperative at all. ... Sure, it was part of the deal that she helped us out, but I don't think she thought that she would end up the same as all her friends. What a bunch of weirdos."

At that, Linny stared at the pantry door in shock, her mind flipping through all the players in this game. The only woman in the bunch was the neighbor lady. *Uh-oh.*

"No, I know. It's a hell of a place here at the compound," he said. "When we take it over, it'll be great, but we haven't taken out all the players yet. We need to get the entire team. If you leave one, they'll come back and kill us. ... No, no, I know. I'll find her. Don't worry. I'll find her. ... Yeah, the guys are in the vehicle. I just came back to double-check her. ... I'll toss her in with the rest of them. ... No, I'm fine. ... Okay, fine. I'll just kill her then. That's probably the easiest anyway. She's proving to be too much of a pain in the ass. Who'd have thought all those guys were after her for her photographs? ... Yeah, like I said, they're all just a few bricks short of a load. ... Yeah, right. I'll be out of here in a few minutes. I've just got to run her down."

And, with that, he hung up the phone.

Linny buried her face in her knees, as she tried to figure out what was going on. But she had an ugly thought in the back of her head. She heard Ice.

"Don't make a sound. That guy's coming for you."

"Maybe I should let him take me," she said. "At least that way we'll find the others."

"No," she snapped. "Didn't you hear him? He'll take you out to make it easier."

"I heard him," she said, as she took a slow deep breath. "I'm in the pantry."

"Weapons?"

She looked around and said, "A set of steak knives are here."

"Open them up and get yourself some," she said. "Not ideal but it's something."

"Also a cleaver," she said.

"Much better," Ice said. "The thing is, if he takes it away from you, he could chop you up with it."

"If I'm dead, I probably won't care," she said, her voice getting slightly hysterical.

"Which won't help at all," she said, "because, when Fallon gets back there, imagine how he'll feel."

That comment steadied her. "Right," she said. "He'll be pissed."

"Exactly. How could he not be?" Ice said. "The thing is, this is just the way life works. What we have to do now is ensure we get you out of there safe and sound."

Listening to Ice's calm voice, patient and pragmatic as always, grounded her. Linny smiled and said, "I can't believe you do this all the time."

"Well, I don't get attacked all the time," she said. "But it's happened more than enough times that we're a little bit too accustomed to it."

"Fine," she whispered. As she looked around, she said, "There's also a cast-iron fry pan."

"Good," Ice said encouragingly. "Cleaver and cast iron. The cast iron will be heavy, but, if you get one solid whack in with that, you'll knock him out or, at the very least, stun him."

"Well, I'll go for knocking him out first. If he hurt anybody here, with the second blow I'll smash his brains in." Just then she heard a gunshot. "Oh, my God," Linny whispered. "Was that gunfire?"

"Yep," Ice said.

"I don't know what to do."

"You stay hidden," Ice ordered. "It's too early for the guys I sent to be there."

"Great," she said. "So now what?" Again she heard footsteps coming back in. She sank back down into her corner, whispering, "He's here again."

"Cast-iron fry pan, cleaver," Ice said.

The pantry door opened, and the guy called out, "Where are you? It's almost like you think I might hurt you or something." Raucous laughter filled the pantry.

She just stopped and held her breath.

He walked into the pantry, turned around, and said, "God damn, she's got to be here somewhere. I don't have time for these damn bitches."

His phone rang again. He pulled it out and said, "No, I

can't find her, goddammit. ... Yes, I already killed the other one. It seemed easier than having to listen to her whining about wanting to go to her boyfriend. I told her that I would take her there. What she didn't know was that I would have to take her to the morgue because that's where he is too. ... Yeah, yeah, yeah, I know. I know. ... Okay, fine, but I can't leave her alive, so I've got to find her."

At that, Linny sank down farther; something beside her shifted, making a noise.

He froze, pocketed his phone, suddenly spun around, dropped down, and saw her. He grinned. "Now there you are. That wasn't that hard, was it?" he said. "All you had to do was let me know earlier, and you would have saved me a ton of aggravation."

At that, he grabbed her arm, his grip latched onto her wrist, almost crushing her bones. Screaming, even as she came out, she swung with all her might and raised the cast-iron frying pan as high as she could and clipped him on the side of the head.

It wasn't enough of a blow to knock him out, but he stumbled backward, releasing her hand and screaming at her. "Bitch!"

The cleaver had already landed on the floor. She kept the cast iron skillet with her, and maybe should have turned around and given him a second whack, but he was already after her. She ran, then slipped into another closet, waiting until he dashed past. Then she turned and came back the opposite way, going for the glass doors outside to the pool area, and bolted for the greenery outside. He came out behind her, having heard her somewhere along the line, firing randomly. They had acres here, and, if she could just get a lead on him, she could take off into the boondocks. But she didn't want to take a chance of getting shot.

When he stopped firing, he called out, "Do you think you'll really get away from me? You damn bitch, you almost crushed my head. I want payback."

Good, asshole. She wanted to yell it out but didn't dare because she didn't want to piss him off any further or reveal her position. When he did get ahold of her, if he did, things would get beyond ugly. Still, as she hunkered down and tried to hide under the tree, he kept swearing and cussing as he stormed through the forest around her. It wasn't that dense, and Bullard sometimes used it for part of his training. She had been around here a lot, but this guy was swinging closer and closer, and she knew it wouldn't be long before he found her. She tightened her grip around the handle of the frying pan, wondering how she could beat up this bastard.

She had had a certain amount of hand-to-hand combat training, but he had at least seventy pounds on her and quite a few inches in height. His reach was longer, and he was one mean son of a bitch. Plus, he was armed. Regardless he had only one thing on his mind right now, and that was taking her down. Well, she only had one thing on her mind too. If her men were in some damn vehicle, she would search for them or would die trying.

Just as he came around her hiding space, she swung her cast iron skillet with all her might, smacked him hard on the kneecap. He went down screaming, his hand pulling the trigger of the handgun as he fired consistently in her area. She dodged and circled the man on his one good knee, swung the cast iron pan and slammed it against his head again and again and again. When she could finally draw a breath, she stopped and stumbled backward.

She realized then that she had crushed his skull. "Oh,

my God. Oh, my God. Oh, my God," she whispered.

He was still alive. She kicked his hand and got away from him, staring, not even sure the doctor in her wanted to save his life. The terrified woman in her wanted to slam him again with the cast iron skillet. She froze.

Ice called out to her through the phone, "Are you okay?"

"Oh, my God," she said. "I didn't kill him, but I've crushed his skull."

"Good," Ice said. "Part of me says you should hit him one more time, but if you think he won't get up and come after you, see if you can secure him to make sure he can't come up after you later. Then you need to find our guys."

"I don't even know what to do with this guy," she said.

"Send me a picture," Ice said.

Linny quickly sent Ice a picture of him.

"Don't worry about him," she said gently. "Get back into the house, and look for the Fallon and Quinn."

"I think he said the garage, didn't he?"

"He said the car actually, but we have to know if the car is in the yard or in the driveway. Where is it?"

She bolted out to the front yard and said, "A vehicle's parked outside."

"Outside the gate?"

"Yes." She walked up to the car quietly. "Nobody in the front seat."

"It did sound like he was alone," Ice said. "Cautiously open the door of the driver's seat, then pull the trunk lever and see if that will open up."

She sat down and tried to find the lever that would open the trunk. And as soon as she did, and it opened, she raced around to the trunk.

"Ice, it's empty," she cried out in distress.

"That's fine," she said. "Are the keys there?"

"I don't know."

"Look for them," Ice said, her voice as calm as ever. "We need to know we can get you out of there."

"I'm not leaving without the guys."

"You'll leave without the men," she said, "if that's what we have to do."

Linny realized that the keys were in the ignition. "The keys are here, but another vehicle is arriving. Somebody's coming."

"Can you get in and drive away fast?"

"No, I'm already under the car."

"Stay there then," she said. "It's probably somebody coming to help him."

"Jesus," she said. "Where are your people?"

"About ten minutes out," she said.

"Who's coming?"

"Don't worry about it," she said. "It's another one of Fallon's team."

"Good," she said, burying her hands underneath. Just then two vehicles came to a ripping stop, and dust clogged her throat.

One man got out of each car.

"Go find that asshole," said one of them. "I'll stay here with the men."

At that, Linny perked up.

She heard Ice in her ear. "Stay quiet."

Linny watched as one of the men took off toward the main house. She waited until he'd gone inside, and then the second man came around near her and said on his phone, "I don't know what the hell you're talking about," he said. "This guy that you brought on board is an idiot. ... I get that," he said. "But you haven't taken over Bullard's company or Kingdom Securities yet, and, so far, the men you got working for you seem like absolute idiots. ... I don't know where this guy was, but he couldn't find and handle one single woman, and, well, that's just stupid. ... Yeah, I know we'll have to pop him, when he gets back out here. Failure's not an option. ... No, I sent Jimmy in," he said. "I'm not going in. I'm keeping an eye on these guys. ... I know, I know. They're in the trunk, that's all."

One of the vehicles had pulled farther up. She peered underneath just in time to see the back of the trunk snap and pop open. But it was grabbed and held down again. From inside.

She smiled.

The guy on the phone turned, watching the house as he talked, walking a little bit farther away. "He should be out in a few minutes. ... No, I'm not going in. I'm not leaving these guys. I'll sit here and wait."

As she watched, he leaned over the hood of the car that he had driven in and said, "It can't be too long."

She watched in horror, her throat completely closing off as she watched Fallon slide out of the trunk. Just as the one guy straightened to turn around, his chin went directly into Fallon's right hook. The stranger stopped, made a gurgling sound, and Fallon quickly snatched the phone from his hand and gave him almost a comical push, and the guy fell to his knees.

"Now," Fallon said into the phone, "I'm coming after you, asshole." With that, he hung up the phone and pocketed it.

She went to slide back out, when Ice urgently said, "Wait. There's still a guy in the house."

Just as she said this, shots rang out. Quinn, now out of the trunk too, and Fallon immediately dropped to the ground for safety; at least she hoped that was why. She stayed under the car, her face buried flat in her arms. She looked to see Fallon staring at her in surprise. She gave him a big grin and a tiny finger wave. He gave her a smile that absolutely melted her heart. Relief came over his face as he realized she was safe.

The second guy came racing up to the vehicles.

"Who the fuck did this?" He reached his buddy and gave him a hard shake, just as Quinn got up and slammed him over the head. Fallon joined Quinn, and together they tackled the big guy. His gun went off, before it was kicked away. Quinn stepped back, gave him a hard right, and he went down. This time, he stayed down.

Fallon called to her, "Linny, it's okay to come out now."

She slid out from underneath the car, held up her phone, and said, "Ice is on the line."

"Good," he said, as he nudged the phone from her hand. "Ice, we're here. We've got both of them. I'll send you pictures."

"Glad to hear that," she said. "Help is on the way."

"Good," he said. "Because, all of a sudden, I'm not feeling too good."

He stared at Linny in surprise and slowly sank to his knees. Then, right in front of her, he pitched headfirst to the ground.

WHEN FALLON WOKE up, he felt himself being jostled, as he was picked up and carried. "Goddammit," he muttered. "Let me go," and he started to struggle.

Somebody grabbed his chin. Then Linny said, "Don't struggle, Fallon. You've been shot, and I need to take out the bullet. We're heading into the surgery."

"Linny, are you okay?" he asked. He felt the waves of grisly pain, fighting against the panic in his heart at her voice.

"I'm fine," she whispered. "I'm fine, but you aren't."

"That's okay," he said. "As long as you are."

"No, damn it, it's not," she snapped. "Now, will you just be quiet?"

"Bossy," he said. "I like that."

He felt a kiss, gentle as a breeze, on his forehead. "I'm glad you do," she said, "because I'm not changing now."

"Neither am I. Remember?"

"No," she said. "I remember just fine. Now would you please be quiet?"

With that, he was put down on a bed of some kind. But hard.

He shifted and cried out.

"See? I told you," she said. "You've been shot. I'm taking care of it. Now hush so I can get you under anesthesia."

But Fallon wouldn't go under. The pain kept waking him up. Finally he heard voices above him, and then somebody gripped the nerve center on his neck. He looked up to see Quinn, saying, "Sorry, buddy." Then Fallon was out cold.

When he woke up the next time, it was to more pain and a sharp agonizing cut into his shoulder. And again Quinn looked at him, smiled, and said, "Time for another nap." Then he did the same pincher move on his neck. Gratefully Fallon went under. When he woke the third time, it was to sunshine. He rolled his head to the side to see Linny sleeping, curled up at his feet. He shifted his feet, trying not to wake her.

But immediately she bounced up, looked at him, and said, "You're awake."

"If that's what you call it," he said. "I feel like I've been shot."

She chuckled. "Well, that's because you were."

"Good, I think," he said. "I'd hate to feel this bad after just a rough night."

"Well, it depends on what we were doing," she said, with a cheeky grin.

He smiled and reached out a hand. "I presume you saved me?"

"Well, you probably would have made it to the hospital," she said, "but you were bleeding pretty badly."

"So we'll just say that you saved me. I'm sure you'll probably regret it down the road."

"I won't regret it down the road," she said instantly. She leaned over and kissed him ever-so-gently. "But I will tell you that you're not going anywhere for a while."

"I'm not giving up now that we're so close," he said.

"We're even closer than you know," she said, "because I heard the one guy talking on the phone. He said something about not having taken over either Bullard's company or Kingdom Securities yet."

"Right, but we don't have a location." Just then he heard several sets of footsteps.

"Actually we do," Quinn said. "I'm staying here. Ryland is here to pick up the slack, what with your injuries."

"Are you sure about the location?" Fallon asked.

"Yeah, I'm pretty sure," he said. "At least I'm waiting for confirmation. Chances are one faction may still be here, but one more active one may be in France, so you might have to run command central for us from here."

"I can do that," he said, trying to shift himself a bit, smiling up at Ryland. "Good to see you. I'll be out of here soon."

"You're not doing anything for a while." Linny turned to Quinn and said, "Don't even start with me."

"Hey, Dave's on his way back," he said, "or at least that's what he said the last I heard from him."

"Actually he sent me a message, saying he had one more person to check out," she said. "So here we were, arguing back and forth, so I told him to go check it out."

"Well, that's great," he said. "But we need more team members then. We're losing them one by one."

"You haven't lost any of them," Linny snapped. "We're all here."

"I'll be fine," Fallon said. "Just let me get up out of bed."

"You're not getting up out of that bed for at least forty-eight hours," she said firmly. "So don't give me any more grief about it."

He looked at her, and an intimate smile slipped across his face. "Are you staying with me?"

"Maybe, if that's what it takes," she said, chuckling.

"So how did this happen while I was away?" Ryland asked, eyeing the two of them.

She looked up at him, smiled, and said, "He doesn't even know that you're here. Not really. He's too out of it yet."

Ryland looked at his buddy and said, "Hey, Fallon, I'm here. Looks like it's your turn to lie low. And, by the way, we've got a few other guys coming in too."

"That's just bullshit," he said. "We got this. And you

aren't recovered," Fallon said. "No way you should be back
on active duty."

"Well, you can try and argue with the rest of us all you
want, but it won't do you any good," Quinn said.

"Damn it," Fallon said, as he stretched back out again.
"Fine, but it's not like you to have things up in the air. Like
it might be Paris, or it might be here."

Just then Quinn's phone rang. He headed off to answer
it, and, when he came back, his face was grim. "We'll go do
some reconnaissance," he said. "Fallon, you've got twenty-
four hours to get back on your feet." Quinn turned and
looked at Linny and said, "At the very least, that's when
we've got men coming in. In the meantime we have some
things to clean up on our own."

She smiled, nodded, and said, "Fine, we need to put an
end to this—and fast."

"Oh, we're on it," Quinn said. "Chances are we're at the
last step now. We just got an address from the phone Fallon
took off one of our shooters, tracking back the last number
dialed. Got his contact list. Everybody's been tracking down
as many of those numbers as we can. But one of them is in
town here."

"Good," Linny said. "Go get 'em."

Quinn looked at her, hesitated, and then walked over
and gave her a big hug, saying, "I know you are hell on
wheels, girl, but make sure you take care of this guy, until
he's able to take care of you."

She kissed Quinn gently on the cheek and said, "Don't
worry about us. We got this." Fallon reached out to grab her
hand. He reiterated her words and said, "I'll stay long
enough to get healed, but, Ryland, as long as you're here, go
with Quinn and see if anybody else is coming back."

"Everybody's coming back," Ryland said. "The show-down will happen, and it'll happen fast. But we need to know all the players before we can get everything sorted out."

"You go do that," he said. "Don't mind me if I catch a nap now, while I can."

With that, the two men disappeared.

EPILOGUE

QUINN SANTOR HEADED out to the garage, looked at the vehicles, and grabbed the large armored vehicle with double-pane bulletproof glass. Ryland hopped in without a word. "Are you sure you're okay to do this? You were hurt pretty badly."

"You're not going without me, buddy," Ryland said. "There's been somebody new in this deal every step of the way, but, at this point in time, I'm here, and the rest of the team is coming home. Let's make sure we get this locked down, so none of us are targets anymore."

At that, Quinn looked at him, smiled, and said, "Sounds good to me."

"You said you got the address. Do you have any other information?"

"Not much. The apartment belongs to a woman," Quinn said.

"Do we know what woman?"

"Yep," he said. "We do, indeed." Ryland turned to look at him with a question in his eyes, and Quinn provided the answer. "It's Isabella's place."

Ryland stopped and stared. "No way Isabella would betray Bullard."

"I know," Quinn said. "So I'm not sure what's going on, but I suggest we find out."

Quinn drove through the double gates and Ryland said, "You believe that, don't you?"

Quinn nodded. "Yeah, I do believe that," he said. "Bullard saved her life, put her through school, and has treated her like a daughter. So, no, I don't think it's her. But I do think it's somebody close to her."

"But that's the problem," Ryland said. "Nobody's close to her, certainly nobody who's connected to Kingdom Securities."

"That's what we have to figure out," Quinn said. He turned and looked at Ryland as he drove down the road. "When was the last time anybody contacted her?"

"I'm not sure," Ryland replied. "What are you thinking?"

"I'm wondering if she's even alive, or if somebody has conveniently made good use of her home because she's not even there."

Ryland's expression clouded. "That wouldn't be good," he said. "But it makes sense, if somebody hates Bullard that badly, they'll hate everybody around him. Particularly somebody he really cares about."

"And that's why we're going there first," Quinn said. "Are you ready?"

Ryland smiled and said, "Always." He prepared to face the next challenge. "What exactly is the relationship between Isabella and Bullard?" Ryland asked.

"She's his half-brother's daughter," Quinn said.

"And the half-brother's dead, correct?"

"No, Bullard's half-brother was a captive for five years, before Bullard managed to track down his location and rescue him. A five-year period where the family had been to hell and back."

Ryland had been with Bullard for a long time, but this wasn't a subject the man cared to talk about.

"He often refers to her as his adopted daughter," Quinn said.

"So Bullard took over Isabella's care when she was little."

"*Little* is relative. She was already fourteen or fifteen, I think. Is that right?" He paused, confirming the time frame. "Right, so she was already a little bit disgruntled over the move, and she hadn't gotten along that well with her father. Then her father was captured."

"But the relationship between her and Bullard was good?" Ryland asked.

"That's my understanding, although I rarely saw them together. So I don't know how good. Honestly, we saw an awful lot more of her when living with Dave."

"Right," Ryland said. "Well, let's go see what we've got." They pulled up outside Isabella's apartment. "Is this it? It's pretty nondescript."

"It's the last address I have on file," Quinn said, puzzled, as he stared at the complex that looked pretty downtrodden. "Though this is not where I would expect her to live."

"Doesn't mean she's actually living here," Ryland said.

"No, that's true. But, at the same time, we have to go by what we have, and this is it, though it doesn't make sense."

"It doesn't. I can't see any family member of Bullard's living here."

"Maybe they aren't as close as I thought," Quinn said.

"Which makes her somebody of interest perhaps."

"Not necessarily," he said.

"We can't give her a pass just because she's family, not until we know more," Ryland said.

"We're not," Quinn said. "What about the rest of the

team? What are they up to?"

"Right now, they're trying to run down Isabella's latest movements," Ryland said. "Of course they're also still tidying up the mess you guys just went through, as they're all trying to get home."

"Are they *all* coming home?"

"Yep, if I had to leave my boat," he said, "you can bet everybody's coming home."

"What about your partner?"

"Tabi's gone back to her home. I didn't want to persuade her to stay there, but, when she understood what we were up to, she was okay with it."

"She doesn't seem like the type to be okay with it."

"I explained that I would be heading out on a mission, so she understood."

"Lucky you," he said.

"Absolutely. I'm the luckiest guy in the world," Ryland muttered. "I still can't believe she cares as much for me as I care for her."

"And there's nothing quite like the scenario you've already been through to highlight all the danger and to make you realize just what's important in life."

"Exactly," Ryland said. "It's all good though. And she's totally okay to be there temporarily."

"Will you bring her back to the compound?"

"We're discussing options," he said, laughing. "She's a nurse."

"Well, if we can get Linny to come over and run Bullard's clinic," he said, "we'll need a nurse."

Ryland looked at him in surprise. "Wow," he said. "I didn't even think Lindsey would be interested in that. What is she looking at doing?"

"Sounds like she's a matter of a few months from getting her general surgery credentials, and you can bet that Fallon's trying to get her to land here."

He chuckled at that. "Now that makes sense. And those two, they're really an item?"

"Finally."

"I know, right? After all that bickering? The last time I was here, and they both were around, I wanted to just lock them up in a room, until they got it out of their system."

Quinn chuckled. "You're not the only one, and they weren't very amiable to such a concept. But they got there eventually."

"Good. That should make Fallon want to live here too."

"Yes, especially right now. He's pretty soft and malleable."

At that, they had a great chuckle at their friend's expense.

Ryland parked on the street. Quinn said, "It's bad enough of a neighborhood that I almost don't want to leave the vehicle here."

"Well, this one we can leave quite happily," he said. "Any of the others, I'm not so sure about."

"Right. Still pretty rough to see this though."

"It is. But let's go see if she's here."

Quinn pulled out his phone to check the address, then said, "She's on the third floor." Shaking his head at that and still not quite believing the circumstances here, they got out and locked up the vehicle. They headed up to the apartment. There was no elevator.

Ryland swore at that. "Good thing it's only the third floor."

"What's the matter? Didn't you eat your Wheaties?"

Quinn teased.

Ryland snorted. "I did, but some of the injuries are still a little stiff," he said, glaring at him. "I'm fine," he said. "So don't try sending me back."

"Like hell," Quinn growled. "You should take the time you need to heal up completely."

"Everybody is coming home," he said, "and it seems like most are dinged up, to one degree or another, so don't get your panties in a twist. We'll all be here to make sure we all get through whatever's going on. The problem is, whatever is going on, makes no sense at all," he said.

"You would think that it would have been a lot easier to run down."

"Too many people involved," he said.

"That's the truth."

So, as they made their way up the stairs, Quinn entered the third-floor hallway and immediately wrinkled his nose.

"Wow," he said. "It seriously reeks in here."

"Not exactly an awe-inspiring place to live, is it?"

"It's disgusting."

Quinn glared at the surroundings, as they found the number on the door. With a shake of his head, he rapped hard on the wood, which seemed to be rotting in its frame. When he got no answer, he looked at Ryland, then knocked again. On the third time, they still got no answer, but somebody across the way opened the door and glared at them.

"If nobody answers, nobody's home," he said. "Are you freaking stupid?" It was some young guy with his hair standing up on end, looking like a Mohawk that may have been wonderful the previous night, but it was now showing the decay of a rough night.

"Do you know who lives here?"

"So, let me get this straight. You're waking me the hell up, and you don't even know whose door you're knocking on?"

Quinn wanted to shake him by the neck and rattle something loose, but instead he asked, "We know who we thought was living here, but it doesn't look like an area we thought she'd be in."

"She? Dude, no woman lives there. You need to get your information updated."

"Well, we're trying to," Ryland said, exasperated. "So can you give us a hand or not?"

"It's a guy," he said, as if that explained everything.

"Do you know what guy?"

"No clue, I think it's her old boyfriend."

"Who's *her*?

"Jesus," he said. "Isabella, of course."

"Well, that's good. That's who we're looking for."

"Well, she's not here," the guy said, completely unhelpful.

"Do you know where we'd find her?"

"Nope, once she let that idiot move in, she pretty well had to move out."

"Do you know how long ago?"

"A long time ago," he said. "I don't know, man, I can't keep track of time."

"Okay, you got anything else you can tell us? About where she went, where she works, anything?"

"What do you want her for? She's a nice girl, and you shouldn't be bothering her."

"If she's a nice girl, what's she doing here?"

"It was the boyfriend," he said. "I don't think she realized what she was in for, but you know? That's what happens, and our slumlord's been making this place a hell of a lot worse, every step of the way."

"She didn't have to stay in a place like this though, did she?"

"Hell if I know," he said. "I didn't know her that well."

"Did you know the boyfriend?"

"Yeah, a loser. He still owes me money. So, if you find him, tell him that he still owes me twenty bucks."

"Well, I will, but who should I say he owes it to?"

The guy snorted. "It's Ozzie, man."

"Ozzie, okay, great," Quinn said, nodding his head.

The guy snorted again and walked back into his apartment and slammed the door.

At that, Quinn turned and looked at Ryland. "Nice area."

"You think?" he said. "Not exactly what I would call a nice area."

"Nope, but still she's not here, so where the hell did she go? And where's this guy?"

"He didn't give us a name, did he?"

"No." They looked at each other, looked at the door to Isabella's, and Quinn quickly picked the lock, letting them in. Immediately the smell hit his nose. "Good God, I wonder if he ever cleaned this mess."

"Probably not since Isabella left, which was a long time ago, whatever that means," Ryland said, with half a sneer.

"This place might have been nice, at one time. But it's been a very long time."

"You can't do much if you're poor," Ryland said.

"Just because you're poor doesn't mean you have to live like a slob. Looks to me like this guy just lives like this because he's too lazy not to."

"Well, let's take a look."

They quickly went through the kitchen and the small bedroom. Outside of the fact that the place was filthy throughout, not a whole lot to be found.

"No mail is even here, nothing identifies anybody, so what the hell is going on here?"

"He ditched this place. That is what happened," Quinn said, as they walked back into the bedroom. Then they stopped and stared.

"So what's that on the walls?" Ryland asked.

"Handcuffs," Quinn said.

"Handcuffs," Ryland repeated, and then he whistled. "So is this just for fun and games?"

"I don't know. But I don't like it."

"But we can't judge them for their sexual activity."

"As long as it was agreeable to both parties, no," Quinn said. "But we can't tell that yet." He walked closer, took a look at the handcuffs on the wall, and whispered. "I wish I had my tool kit here."

"Why? What do you see?"

"These cuffs are covered with dried blood."

This concludes Book 6 of Bullard's Battle: Fallon's Flaw.

Read about Quinn's Quest: Bullard's Battle, Book 7

Quinn's Quest: Bullard's Battle (Book #7)

Welcome to a new stand-alone but interconnected series from Dale Mayer. This is Bullard's story—and that of his team's. All raw, rough, incredibly capable men who have one goal: to find out who was behind the attack on their leader, before the attacker, or attackers, return to finish the job.

Stay tuned for more nonstop action as the men narrow down their suspects ... and find a way to let love back into their own empty lives.

Fed up with always feeling one step behind, Quinn is determined to find out who is trying to annihilate all of Bullard's team. Only the trail takes him to Izzie, Bullard's niece. The team knows the saboteur was someone close to Bullard, and Izzie had had a hell of a fight with Bullard the last time they spoke. But how involved was she in this plane crash? He didn't want to think badly of her, but, at this point in time, he was looking at everyone with suspicion.

Izzie is also suspicious of everyone. She's been to hell and back, all because she was stubborn and angry at Bullard, but she'd never do anything to hurt him. Not knowing anything about the last few months' trials, she's horrified to find out why Quinn sought her out. Then he's horrified when he finds out what happened to her. Working on healing her own soul, she's desperate to help Quinn find out who attacked the team and potentially killed her uncle.

If she can do anything to help, she will, particularly if it gives her a chance to make amends to the one man who's always been there for her.

Find Book 7 here!

To find out more visit Dale Mayer's website.

smarturl.it/DMSQuinn

Damon's Deal: Terkel's Team (Book #1)

Welcome to a brand-new series from *USA Today* best-selling author Dale Mayer, where dark-ops SEALs have special senses and skills, needed to solve intrigue, betrayal, and ... murder. A series with all the elements you've come to love, plus so much more, ... including psychics!

ICE POURED HERSELF a coffee and sat down at the compound's massive dining room table with the others. When her phone rang, she smiled at the number displayed. "Hey, Terk. How're you doing?" She put the call on Speakerphone.

"I'm okay," Terkel said, his voice distracted and tight.

"Terk?" Merk called from across the table. He got up and walked closer and sat across from Levi. "You don't sound too good, brother. What's up?"

"I'm fine," Terk said. "Or I will be. Right now, things are blown to shit."

"As in literally?" Merk asked.

"The entire group," Terk said, "they're all gone. I had a

solid team of eight, and they're all gone."

"Dead?"

Several others stood to join them, gathered around Ice's phone. Levi stepped forward, his hand on Ice's shoulder. "Terk? Are they all dead?"

"No." Terk took a deep breath. "I'm not making sense. I'm sorry."

"Take it easy," Ice said, her voice calm and reassuring. "What do you mean, *they're all gone?*"

"All their abilities are gone," he said. "Something's happened to them. Somebody has deliberately removed whatever super senses they could utilize—or what we have been utilizing for the last ten years for the government." His tone was bitter. "When the US gov recently closed us down, they promised that our black ops department would never rise again, but I didn't expect them to attack us personally."

"What are you talking about?" Merk said in alarm, standing up now to stare at Ice's phone. "Are you in danger?"

"Maybe? I don't know," Terk said. "I need to find out exactly what the hell's going on."

"What can we do to help?" Ice asked.

Terk gave a broken laugh. "That's not why I'm calling. Well, it is, but it isn't."

Ice looked at Merk, who frowned, as he shook his head. Ice knew he and the others had heard Terk's stressed out tone and the completely confusing bits and pieces coming from his mouth. Ice said, "Terk, you're not making sense again. Take a breath and explain. Please. You're scaring me."

Terk took a long slow deep breath. "Tell Stone to open the gate," he said. "She's out there."

"Who's out there?" Levi asked, hopped up, looked outside, and shrugged.

"She's coming up the road now. You have to let her in."

"Who? Why?"

"*Because*," he said, "she's also harnessed with C-4."

"Jesus," Levi said, bolting to display the camera feeds to the big screen in the room. "Is it live?"

"It is, and she's been sent to you."

"Well, that's an interesting move," Ice said, her voice sharp, activating her comm to connect to Stone in the control room. "Who's after us?"

"I think it's rebels within the Iranian government. But it could be our own government. I don't know anymore," Terk snapped. "I also don't know how they got her so close to you. Or how they pinned your connection to me," he said. "I've been very careful."

"We can look after ourselves," Ice said immediately. "But who is this woman to you?"

"She's pregnant," he said, "so that adds to the intensity here."

"Understood. So who is the father? Is he connected somehow?"

There was silence on the other end.

Merk said, "Terk, talk to us."

"She's carrying my baby," Terk replied, his voice heavy.

Merk, his expression grim, looked at Ice, her face mirroring his shock. He asked, "How do you know her, Terk?"

"Brother, you don't understand," Terk said. "I've never met this woman before in my life." And, with that, the phone went dead.

Find Book 1 here!

To find out more visit Dale Mayer's website.

smarturl.it/DMSTTDamon

Author's Note

Thank you for reading Fallon's Flaw: Bullard's Battle, Book 6! If you enjoyed the book, please take a moment and leave a short review.

Dear reader,

I love to hear from readers, and you can contact me at my website: www.dalemayer.com or at my Facebook author page. To be informed of new releases and special offers, sign up for my newsletter or follow me on BookBub. And if you are interested in joining Dale Mayer's Reader Group, here is the Facebook sign up page.
https://smarturl.it/DaleMayerFBGroup

Cheers,
Dale Mayer

Get THREE Free Books Now!

Have you met the SEALS of Honor?

SEALs of Honor Books 1, 2, and 3. Follow the stories of brave, badass warriors who serve their country with honor and love their women to the limits of life and death.

Read Mason, Hawk, and Dane right now for FREE.

Go here and tell me where to send them!
http://smarturl.it/EthanBofB

About the Author

Dale Mayer is a *USA Today* best-selling author, best known for her SEALs military romances, her Psychic Visions series, and her Lovely Lethal Garden cozy series. Her contemporary romances are raw and full of passion and emotion (Broken But ... Mending series). Her thrillers will keep you guessing (By Death series), and her romantic comedies will keep you giggling (*It's a Dog's Life*, a stand-alone novella; and the Broken Protocols series, starring Charming Marvin, the cat).

Dale honors the stories that come to her—and some of them are crazy and break all the rules and cross multiple genres!

To go with her fiction, she also writes nonfiction in many different fields, with books available on résumé writing, companion gardening, and the US mortgage system. She has recently published her Career Essentials series. All her books are available in print and ebook format.

Connect with Dale Mayer Online

Dale's Website – www.dalemayer.com
Twitter – @DaleMayer
Facebook – facebook.com/DaleMayer.author
BookBub – bookbub.com/authors/dale-mayer

Also by Dale Mayer

Published Adult Books:

Bullard's Battle

Ryland's Reach, Book 1

Cain's Cross, Book 2

Eton's Escape, Book 3

Garret's Gambit, Book 4

Kano's Keep, Book 5

Fallon's Flaw, Book 6

Quinn's Quest, Book 7

Bullard's Beauty, Book 8

Bullard's Best, Book 9

Terkel's Team

Damon's Deal, Book 1

Kate Morgan

Simon Says... Hide, Book 1

Hathaway House

Aaron, Book 1

Brock, Book 2

Cole, Book 3

Denton, Book 4

The K9 Files

Lovely Lethal Gardens

Psychic Vision Series

Tuesday's Child

Hide 'n Go Seek

Maddy's Floor

Garden of Sorrow

Knock Knock…

Rare Find

Eyes to the Soul

Now You See Her

Shattered

Into the Abyss

Seeds of Malice

Eye of the Falcon

Itsy-Bitsy Spider

Unmasked

Deep Beneath

From the Ashes

Stroke of Death

Ice Maiden

Snap, Crackle…

What If…

Psychic Visions Books 1–3

Psychic Visions Books 4–6

Psychic Visions Books 7–9

By Death Series

Touched by Death

Haunted by Death

Chilled by Death

By Death Books 1–3

Broken Protocols – Romantic Comedy Series
Cat's Meow

Cat's Pajamas

Cat's Cradle

Cat's Claus

Broken Protocols 1-4

Broken and... Mending
Skin

Scars

Scales (of Justice)

Broken but... Mending 1-3

Glory
Genesis

Tori

Celeste

Glory Trilogy

Biker Blues
Morgan: Biker Blues, Volume 1

Cash: Biker Blues, Volume 2

SEALs of Honor
Mason: SEALs of Honor, Book 1

Hawk: SEALs of Honor, Book 2

Dane: SEALs of Honor, Book 3

Swede: SEALs of Honor, Book 4

SEALs of Steel

The Mavericks

Lennox, Book 10

Gavin, Book 11

Shane, Book 12

Diesel, Book 13

Jerricho, Book 14

Killian, Book 15

The Mavericks, Books 1–2

The Mavericks, Books 3–4

The Mavericks, Books 5–6

The Mavericks, Books 7–8

The Mavericks, Books 9–10

The Mavericks, Books 11–12

Collections

Dare to Be You...

Dare to Love...

Dare to be Strong...

RomanceX3

Standalone Novellas

It's a Dog's Life

Riana's Revenge

Second Chances

Published Young Adult Books:

Family Blood Ties Series

Vampire in Denial

Vampire in Distress

Vampire in Design

Vampire in Deceit

Vampire in Defiance

Vampire in Conflict

Vampire in Chaos

Vampire in Crisis

Vampire in Control

Vampire in Charge

Family Blood Ties Set 1–3

Family Blood Ties Set 1–5

Family Blood Ties Set 4–6

Family Blood Ties Set 7–9

Sian's Solution, A Family Blood Ties Series Prequel
Novelette

Design series

Dangerous Designs

Deadly Designs

Darkest Designs

Design Series Trilogy

Standalone

In Cassie's Corner

Gem Stone (a Gemma Stone Mystery)

Time Thieves

Published Non-Fiction Books:

Career Essentials
Career Essentials: The Résumé

Career Essentials: The Cover Letter

Career Essentials: The Interview

Career Essentials: 3 in 1

Made in the USA
Las Vegas, NV
10 September 2021